A black substance spilled from the crags and began to diffuse, as if underwater. Even with the audio all but muted, Tech could hear a kind of hideous squeal accompanying the outpouring. As he watched, the blackness began to coalesce into the shapes of living things of gruesome aspect. Whatever this thing was, it was of a different order of evil, as much inside his mind as illuminating the inner face of the headset visor. . . .

"We're outnumbered," Harwood said. "We need speed. Marz, enable Turbo seven-five. Get us moving!"

Disappearing into the conduit, they poured on the speed, ultimately punching through the hatch Harwood had discovered. With their short-lived invulnerability already beginning to fade, they reemerged in the dungeon of Peerless Engineering's castle.

Scaum was waiting for them, metamorphosed into something serpentine and venomous.

Tech's veins filled with ice. . . .

WEB WARRIORS

MEMORIES END

JAMES LUCENO

red sky
publishing

DEL REY

BALLANTINE BOOKS • NEW YORK

A Del Rey® Book
Published by The Ballantine Publishing Group
Copyright © 2002 by Red Sky Entertainment, Inc.

All rights reserved under International and Pan-American Copyright Conventions. Published in the United States by The Ballantine Publishing Group, a division of Random House, Inc., New York, and simultaneously in Canada by Random House of Canada Limited, Toronto.

Del Rey is a registered trademark and the Del Rey colophon is a trademark of Random House, Inc.

www.delreydigital.com

ISBN 0-345-44471-X

Manufactured in the United States of America

First Edition: July 2002

OPM   10 9 8 7 6 5 4 3 2 1

WEB WARRIORS

MEMORIES END

Chapter 1

WEB WARRIORS

Death Run was not for the faint of heart.

The three frequent flyers who had challenged Tech on the racing circuit were already learning that, and falling far behind as a result.

Tech caught a glimpse of them in the rearview window of his headset visor as he shot the Fireball through an abrupt turn and barrel-rolled through a palisade of shock spikes thrust from a low overhang at the last possible moment.

His trio of opponents were piloting flashy vehicles of the sort any novice flyer might design. The one closest to the blazing thrusters of Tech's silver needle-nosed interceptor was a Nighthawk F-117 fighter jet, complete with tinted cockpit canopy and V-shaped tail. To Tech the purple metal-flake fuselage and orange trim said one thing: all show, no go. The pair at the rear of the pack were nearly identical

Stormbird rocket sleds—wedge-shaped vehicles straight off the menu Death Run offered when you entered the course. The sleds' maneuverability made up for their inherent lack of power, but only an experienced flyer could hope to fly a Stormbird to victory.

Angling for clear space, Tech decelerated slightly and allowed the Nighthawk to come alongside him. As the fighter jet edged into first place, Tech paid careful attention to the data displays in his visor, for there was a precise moment when a skillful flyer could borrow speed from an opponent's cybercraft and turn it to his own advantage. When that moment of data drag came, flashing red in the visor, Tech fired his afterburners and leaped back into the lead, surging through a stretch of twitchy S-turns and launching the Fireball over a hidden trap that opened like a yawning tooth-filled mouth.

The Nighthawk didn't fare as well.

Coming out of the last of the tight curves, the sleek-bodied jet overcorrected, tilted up on one wing, and flew directly into the trap. The mouth snapped shut and the teeth gnashed, grinding the ship to fragments, then spit the pieces back onto the course. Mangled jet parts, caroming and careening off the retaining walls, greeted the Stormbirds just as they were emerging from the S-turns.

Tech watched the two rocket sleds attempt to slalom through the tempest only to collide with each other. With loud explosions Tech could feel in his chest, the Stormbirds came apart and disappeared from sight. Stoked on car-shredding, high-adrenaline crashes and multivehicle wrecks, the crowd yelled and hooted. Chuckling to himself, Tech cranked the volume of his speed-metal soundtrack. DisArray blared in his earphones as he entered the final lap of the course full out, whipping through a perilous loop and dropping into a rollercoaster downhill that nearly sent his stomach into his throat.

Even though gravity held sway on the Death Run circuit, you could perform some truly astonishing maneuvers. And Death Run was nothing compared to some of Grand Adventure's other options, where you could log in to space combat scenarios or fast-paced action adventures. On many of those courses, pedestrians wandered out in front of you—not people, but aliens or monsters—and your run could be slowed by out-of-control threesixties on an alien blood slick or end suddenly in a head-on collision with a giant scorpion.

Still more sophisticated runs required you to tear through fantasy worlds, perform power ups at sublight speed, fly by instruments in the dark, or streak through clouds laced with acids that ate away at your craft. The newer courses mimicked actual conditions on Venus or Jupiter or were set on completely fabricated planetscapes, where predatory life-forms could swoop down and pluck you from cinnamon skies.

But weightlessness was for science fiction geeks.

Tech was a fan of gravity if for no other reason than that gravity amplified the hazards, and Death Run was flat-out hard-rock exhilaration. If you weren't lightning fast, you were geek drivel. Add a state-of-the-art motion-capture vest to your flight wardrobe and you could actually *feel* the effects of your accelerations and hairpin turns, the extreme verticality, big-air barrel rolls, and corkscrew flips—not to mention the consequences of losing control and vanishing from the circuit in a roiling ball of fire.

Tech hadn't been looking for a contest when he signed on to Grand Adventure Park fifteen minutes earlier. His goal then had been to test out a piece of software he and his brother had picked up from a dealer who operated out of the Sushi Warehouse downtown. The dealer—an Asian known only as Tsunami—had called it the soft Subterfuge and had touted it as the latest thing in ghost programs. But a race was a race, and Tech had a reputation to uphold.

With the finish line in sight and the odometer display in his visor already counting down the remaining distance, Tech wove the interceptor through another cluster of spike barriers and negotiated a dogleg without surrendering too much momentum. Fishtailing into the homestretch, he poured on speed until the course and the spectators who packed the arena stands became a blur.

Colored lights strobed before his eyes, and applause from the crowd of onlookers threatened to overpower the mega-bass music that thrummed through the headphones. The fact that some people would have been quick to dismiss Death Run as little more than a cleverly engineered illusion didn't diminish the victory or trouble him for even a second, because Tech lived for such moments.

Those same cynics regarded the whole of the Virtual Network—cyberspace, the metaverse, or whatever you liked to call it—to be scarcely more real than a dream. They thought of the Network's multilevel grid of broad avenues and narrow streets, its geometric constructs and public spaces, as nothing more than computer-generated images filling the visor screens they had strapped around their heads to eclipse their view of the real world. A tool to be used like Stock Watch, or disposable entertainment like satellite TV.

But to Tech the Network was much more than that. It was a brave new world, crammed with awesome vehicles, fantastic sights, and endless opportunities. It was an environment more gripping than the real world, governed by its own rules and requirements, and demanding dexterity, cleverness, and skill on the part of all those who took it seriously. Where else, after all, could you soar at the speed of sound through a city that dwarfed any on the planet and experience thrills that were beyond the imaginings of all but the most talented cyber-architects?

In cyberspace honor and glory were up for grabs, and if you were good there, you could write your own future.

"Bulletproof, bro," a voice said, intruding slightly on the fantasy. "New course record."

The voice belonged to Tech's only slightly younger brother, who looked nothing at all like lanky, blond-haired, fifteen-year-old Tech. On the Network, and as often as he could get away with it in the real world, Tech's brother went by the user name Marz—short for Marshall. Marz was a decent cyberflyer himself, but he was a killer navigator and a hardcore designer. While Tech was in the flight chair, all five-feet-five of nut-brown, multi-taskmaster Marz would be at the controls of the cyberconsole monitoring Tech's actions in the Network while simultaneously refining his cybercraft designs, downloading sound samples, and playing air-keys to Global Synth.

"You just placed on the One-to-Beat ranking," Marz added a moment later. "Fearless, man."

Tech accepted the praise without comment. No matter how much you loved to race, it was important to retain an air of nonchalance toward pretty much everything, except for really obscure Japanese games with names Tech could pronounce. After completing his victory lap, he set the interceptor on autopilot.

Death Run was a big win, sure to become the talk of the chat rooms—for a couple of minutes, at any rate. But Tech would have been the first to argue that skilled cyberflying—dazzling flying—was about more than being fearless. Anyone could be dauntless on the courses when the worst fate that could befall a careless racer was a virtual collision or a harsh reprimand by a game master.

Well, maybe your computer system would crash and burn because you had pushed it over the wall, but that only happened to losers. Sure, a racer needed to take risks. But when it came to winning with style, artistry mattered more than raw nerve.

"You ready to get back to work now?" Marz asked carefully.

"Work," Tech said with derision. "Don't you ever think about anything else?"

"Yeah," Marz said, drawing out the word. "But Felix is going to redline if we don't retrieve that file."

Tech grunted in dismissal. "We can find that file with our eyes closed."

"That's what you told Felix three days ago."

Felix was Felix McTurk, the data detective for whom Tech and Marz did occasional fieldwork, and from whose office, on the sixty-fifth floor of the Empire State Building in midtown Manhattan, Tech was flying.

One of countless finders of stolen or misplaced data, Felix's was a struggling, one-man operation. But Felix was pretty chill for an adult, and Data Discoveries paid better than fast food or convenience store work. The missing file Tech and his brother had been instructed to locate belonged to one of Felix's clients—an electrician—who had recently received a phone bill for $505,204.25. The problem was that the electrician's home computer had crashed, and she couldn't prove that she hadn't placed the calls she had been billed for. Normally the phone company would have been able to provide a backup file, but the company's central computer had been befuddled by a virus.

Felix's client was one of many who had received similarly outlandish bills. But the phone-call log that would establish the electrician's innocence was surely somewhere in the Network, misfiled or buried, just waiting for top-gun flyers like Tech and Marz to find and retrieve.

Resigned to his mission, Tech raised the back of the old dentist's chair that was his flight seat and adjusted the fit of his headset visor. He was about to ask his brother to provide him with a craft more suited to a data search when a flying saucer came alongside him, matching the interceptor's speed.

The saucer's unseen pilot hailed him over a Network audio link.

"I've been looking for you," the stranger said.

Tech thought he recognized the voice and took a closer look at the saucer. The opalescent burgundy craft was built for show, but it pulsed with concealed power. It belonged to Bios7, a Network legend with more race wins to his credit than anyone could count. But Tech wasn't about to let his challenger see him sweat.

"Is that supposed to be a flying saucer, Bios7, or a button from the dress you're wearing to the school prom?"

Bios7 laughed. "Actually, it's the bitter pill you're going to have to swallow after you lose to me in a one-on-one."

Bitter pill? Tech thought.

It sounded like a phrase Felix would use, which could mean that Bios7 wasn't Tech's age, but some old dude with a fully tricked-out cybersystem, or maybe even somebody's computer-skilled grandmother logging on from a retirement community in Mexico or somewhere.

You just couldn't help but wonder who some of these people were in the real world, despite what their user profiles stated. So-called experts claimed that the identities people adopted in the Network represented everything they wished they could be in real life. But Tech didn't buy the theory. Network identities were more like funhouse-mirror reflections: the virtual you was just barely askew of the real you. Although in his own case, Tech liked to think that he was the same person in both realms—a born explorer in search of adventure.

"You're getting quite a rep, kid," Bios7 went on. "You think you're ready for the race I have in mind?"

"Try me. I'll understand if you want to keep it private—just so there won't be too many witnesses to your defeat."

"Private's the last place I race, slacker. We run the Ribbon."

The challenge took Tech by surprise. To hackers, cyberjockeys, and frequent flyers, the Ribbon was the Network's Main Street, its Times Square and Sunset Strip. You couldn't get more opposite of private than the Ribbon.

"What's the matter?" Bios7 asked. "Afraid of getting ticketed by Network Security and having your wings clipped?"

"The syscops would have to catch me first," Tech said. "And I haven't been caught yet."

"Then let's do it. Straight down the Ribbon, from CyberSquare to the Peerless Castle. Once around, and back to the strip."

"Uh, Tech," Marz interrupted worriedly. "We don't have time for this. We're already late."

"Ah, your navigator to the rescue," Bios7 teased.

"I can beat this guy," Tech boasted.

"No doubt, Tech," Marz agreed. "So why waste time racing?"

"Racing is never a waste of time," Bios7 said.

"This'll take five minutes," Tech told his brother over a confidential audio channel. "Besides, how's it gonna look if I turn down a challenge from Bios7?"

"Who cares how it's going to look?" Marz said. "We've got work to do."

"And we'll get to it, bro—right after I wipe the smirk off this joker's face."

Marz considered making a stronger argument for not racing, but only for a moment. Competitive runs that pitted seasoned flyers against one another were more about pride than victory. And he knew his brother. There was no changing Tech's mind once he had been dared. So instead Marz took a long swallow of Impact soda and called up a detailed map of the Ribbon. While the map was resolving on the largest of the office's monitor screens, he began loading additional software Tech would need for the race—command, control, and collision-avoidance programs—along with a batch of Tech's favorite music files, most of which were fast, crunching, and loud.

This wouldn't be the first time Tech had raced outside one of the closed circuits, but each race had brought him closer to being flamed by Network Security—the syscops—and getting caught could spell serious trouble for Tech, Marz, and Data Discoveries.

Tech reopened the audio link to Bios7.

"I'll meet you on the Ribbon, chump. Just be thankful we're not racing for system passcodes."

Bios7 laughed heartily. "You're the one who oughta be thankful. You get to lose to the best."

Once more Tech muted the audio feed and swiveled the dentist's chair toward Marz's workstation. "Open the garage," he said with more than a hint of impatience. "I'm going to need some Venom."

Chapter 2

WEB WARRIORS

A database of vehicles designed mostly by Marz, the virtual garage contained more than thirty custom crafts appropriate for everything from racing to off-Ribbon adventuring to certified espionage missions. Some of the ships—like the Fireball Tech had flown in the Death Run challenge—were sleek and aerodynamic looking, while others were deliberately retro and ungainly, intended to attract as little attention as possible. Still others were tributes to ground effect or aerial craft lifted from popular books or blockbuster movies.

If judged by the Network adage that a cyberflyer was only as cool as what he or she piloted, then Tech and Marz would have been in the running for the hippest flyers on the grid.

Tech exited Grand Adventure's volcano-shaped entertainment complex at the controls of the boomerang-shaped Venom, whose crimson luster was every bit as iridescent as that of

Bios7's burgundy saucer. The fingers of his right hand tapped the buttons that studded the batwing control pad affixed to the joystick. With the Network Positioning System enabled, he used the virtual keyboard to enter his destination. It was a bit like typing in the address of some site in the old World Wide Web, but with a couple of major differences. First of all, you got to see every site that was located between your starting point and your destination; and second of all, you *literally* got to see them—fleshed out as constructs of every conceivable design, in full surroundsight, and haloed by other flyers entering, exiting, or simply lurking about with no fixed destination in mind.

Positioned between Grand Adventure and the head of the Ribbon was CyberSquare, a meeting place and hangout for frequent flyers, and sometimes a launch point for illegal races.

Bios7's saucer was parked at the southern perimeter of the square when Tech maneuvered the Venom down to the grid's principal horizontal axis.

"Nice ship," Bios7 quipped. "Does it actually fly?"

"You'll see soon enough," Tech said.

Bios7 snorted. "Our crafts are rated almost equal for endurance and speed. So I say anything goes—malfunctions, pilot errors, oversights."

"Force commands?" Tech asked.

"If you think you can handle them," Bios7 said.

"You'd be surprised what I can handle."

By then word of the one-on-one race had spread through the Network, and untold numbers of spec-

tators were lining up along the Ribbon to watch.
The lots fronting the hot spots and hangouts—
Ziggy's Cyberchop Shop, the Opposite 7,
Sinema—were quickly filling to capacity with
heavily customized cruisers, cybercycles, and other
craft of wide-ranging design. Wagers were being
placed.

To both sides of the broad avenue that was the
Network's commercial zone rose unimaginably tall
towers, some reminiscent of buildings drawn from
old cartoons, and others so detailed you could
swear you were back in the real world. Encased in
plasmascript advertising banners, the towers were
home to dating services, brokerage houses, PG and
adult entertainments, role-playing realms, religious
instruction, martial arts and wrestling matches, TV
shows and movies, music raves, and live chats that
had been going on for years.

Beyond the towers and the deep canyons that
separated them spread a span of cubes, spheres,
and pyramids that were corporate headquarters,
storage facilities, data libraries, and outposts for
syndicate neural nets. Elsewhere were cathedrals,
arenas, and wooded parks.

At the far end of the Ribbon, rising from the
heart of the grid, loomed the fairy-tale castle of
Peerless Engineering, the multinational corporation that had wrested control of the Network from
the cyberwizards who had designed it. Peerless also
had been largely responsible for making the Network accessible to anyone with a cybersystem, a
willingness to explore, and a tolerance for mild
vertigo.

Side by side, Tech and Bios7 moved their craft onto the Ribbon. Tech took a calming breath and told himself to make his hands and feet extensions of his mind.

"You ready, hotshot?" Bios7 asked.

"I was reincarnated ready."

Piloting a lipstick-shaped craft to a position between the Venom and the saucer, a girl named Eye-Catcher counted down from ten and the race began.

Traffic was heavy as the racers shot straight down the center of the Ribbon. Tourists tried to move out of their path, but some weren't quick enough. Tech could only guess at the number of browsers and lurkers he and Bios7 displaced or knocked off-Network in their rapid passing—though Marz could be counted on to furnish him with the exact number at some point after the race.

Navigating the avenues, alleys, overpasses, and tunnels of the Network was similar to moving about in the real world. The speeds you could attain depended on power, timing, traffic flow, and just how much you were willing or able to bend or break the rules. Anyone with a fast machine could perform the equivalent of running yellow or red lights, passing on the inside, slipping into high-occupancy lanes—even though flying solo—or taking advantage of any number of shortcuts. But if you had a really fast machine, loaded to the max with the necessary software, you could not only reach speeds impossible to attain in the real world, you could also overcome some of the protocols that governed movement inside the Network. You could not only pass laterally, but also ascend or descend to other levels, piggyback yourself to other flyers, go *through* buildings as opposed to around them, enter utility shafts, or drop down into the assembler-code corridors that sustained the grid itself.

Tech and Bios7 did all these things as they jinked and juked toward the Peerless Castle. In Tech's headphones the earsplitting chords of Thunder Cracker mixed with the resounding encouragement of spectators parked along the course.

Neck and neck and resolved to disable each other, they hurled commands over their audio link. Bios7 tried for a force skid while Tech was writhing through a dense cluster of frequent flyers, but Tech managed to regain control of his ripped racer and counter with a low-fuel command. The maneuver cost Bios7 precious seconds while he rushed to refresh his ruby saucer by drawing from the power cells of a surprised lurker, and Tech shot into the lead.

At the base of the Peerless Castle, the Ribbon divided into three lanes. The two outer lanes encircled the virtual construct, clock- and counterclockwise, while the middle lane coursed over a broad moat and led directly to the castle's portcullis—its principal gate.

All three lanes were heavily patrolled by security craft, but the central one was also reinforced by antiviral and barrier programs that protected Peerless from acts of cyberterrorism. Peerless was the big kid on the block, but its authority was often being challenged by one start-up company or another. A flyer could find him or herself in deep strife for even venturing too close to Peerless, let alone for trying to outwit the speed filters to race around the castle at top speed.

The plan called for Tech and Bios7 to take the counterclockwise lane and complete one lap around the craggy mountain from which the castle rose. The first to arrive back at the Ribbon would be declared the winner.

Taking advantage of his small lead, Tech whipped the Venom to the right. But just short of the divide, and making it appear as if he had succumbed to one of Bios7's force-head wind commands, he allowed Bios7's saucer to edge alongside him on the inside.

Tech watched his visor displays, waiting for his opponent to accelerate; then, when the two ships were almost even, Tech slipped into the saucer's data drag. At the same time, he nudged Bios7 into the center lane, and shouted, "Force steering lock!"

For a moment, it seemed as if Bios7 had been caught off guard and would have no choice but to shoot across the castle's drawbridge and wrestle with the security patrols stationed there. But at the last instant, the saucer slewed effortlessly back into the right lane and again pulled alongside Tech.

"Nice try, kid," he said, "but you've used that trick once too often."

With a staggering surge of power, the saucer cut diagonally across the blunt nose of the Venom to recapture the lead. Flat out, the two ships tore into the banked curve.

Behind the turreted castle, the grid all but disappeared into a featureless black abyss.

The Escarpment, as it was called, was equivalent to a ten-thousand-foot sheer drop into nothingness. It had been engineered by a group of renegade hackers who had been Peerless's competitors in giving form to the Virtual Network. Peerless had tried on numerous occasions to delete, move, or bridge the abyss, but the company's cybertechnicians had been unable to break the code the hackers had used in creating it.

Had Peerless been successful, the Network would have been able to expand into the Wilds, which lay to the south, far below the castle. But as it was, the Wilds remained a fringe outlaw zone with sites seldom visited by the tourists and shoppers who patronized the Ribbon.

A few daredevil flyers had tried to bridge the abyss in their own fashion by soaring over the edge at top speed. But none were known to have accomplished the jump. While getting nailed by a syscop or a security patrol could not only knock you off-Network but also leave you with a boiled brain and a toasted cybersystem, a plunge into the abyss could render you unconscious or worse.

A third of the way around the embankment, Bios7 began to power down and hug the inside of the curve. It was the safe and sensible thing to do— the only sane way to circumnavigate the castle— and Tech knew that he should follow suit. But he just couldn't bring himself to fall in behind the saucer. In a race like this, you lived or died by taking risks. Instead, he increased his speed, hoping to take Bios7 on the outside.

"Ease up, Tech," Marz warned suddenly. "You can't hold the curve at that speed."

Gritting his teeth, Tech tightened his grip on the joystick but didn't lift his foot from the accelerator. "I can do this, bro. I can do this."

Racing on the grid required deep-immersion techniques, and therefore was universally condemned by the watchdogs of the Network. It had turned the younger generation into Net addicts. It tampered with reality by blurring the distinction between the real and the virtual. And then there were the actual physical dangers associated with the cybersport. Racing threw a flyer's nervous and circulatory systems into overdrive. It stressed the kidneys and adrenal glands, battered the eardrums, and bombarded the optic nerves with images. It tricked the body into activating all sorts of fight-or-flight loops.

And yet Tech ate it up—all of it.

"You sure know how to put on a show, I'll give you that much," Bios7 said as the two ships raced at top speed toward the high point of the embankment.

"Save it," Tech barked, fighting to keep control of his ship. "You can give up now if you want."

The motion-capture vest, which both monitored a flyer's vital signs and enabled a navigator to keep tabs on his pilot, made Tech feel as if he were being crushed against the right side of his cockpit, and the wireless joystick shuddered in sympathy.

"Okay, kid," Bios7 said soberly. "Let me know where you land, *if* you land."

The saucer had just dropped back when the Venom began to spin through a dizzying succession of counterclockwise circles. Tech's hands slipped from the control stick, and he thought he was going to throw up. The castle became a smear in the visor. He tried valiantly to steady himself and his ship, but his best efforts weren't good enough.

The Venom rocketed over the brink of the Escarpment with nowhere to go but down.

"Be seeing you," Bios7 said as Tech plunged into darkness. "In the end you're just another flamer. All show, no go."

WEB WARRIORS

Tech fell in gloom. The joystick felt lifeless in his hand, and the power chords of Thunder Cracker sounded as if they were coming from underwater. He wondered whether he'd simply crash and burn or wake up in a hospital bed, laid low by a case of cyberstupor.

He could almost taste the bitter pill Bios7 had made him swallow.

Then, against all expectation, the Network began to flicker back to life in Tech's visor, and the music returned to normal volume.

Marz's voice cut in. "Are you all right?"

"I think so," Tech said.

"Good. Then I feel okay about calling you a total jackout."

Tech accepted the rebuke. "Stupid, stupid move . . . I had him." He took a long, puzzled look at the featureless spheres and cubes that surrounded him. "Hello, where am I?"

"You're in the Metroplex Enforcement District," Marz said angrily. "I managed to deploy a safety chute just as you were going over the edge."

Tech shook his head in disbelief. "Man, I must have caught a data current. But at least I didn't drop out of the grid, right?"

"Bios7 set a new record for a Ribbon run," Marz took clear pleasure in saying. "He told me to tell you, 'Better luck next time.' "

"*Next* time I'll go with the Mirage," Tech fired back. "At least that one won't skid out from under me."

Marz bristled and started to reply, but thought better of it.

"Hey, Marz . . ."

"Yeah?"

"Thanks, bro."

"Hey, who else is going to keep you in line?"

Marz couldn't help but smile. He ran a hand over his curly brown hair and studied the on-screen map. "You can make a graceful exit back to the Ribbon at the next vertical intersection."

Graceful exits were more for the sake of the flyer than the system. A cyberjockey could always get out of a tight spot by raising his or her headset visor, but such graceless exits were potentially dangerous for deep-immersion flyers like Tech to whom the Network was everything. There were dozens of documented cases of temporary blindness and/or psychosis resulting from "pulling the plug."

"Once you hit the Ribbon, I'll give you a new course heading," Marz continued. "I've got a clearer echo of the electrician's telephone file. The file's hung up in one of AmTel's relay stations. Shouldn't be too difficult to grab. Fact, if we hurry, we can retrieve the thing before Felix gets to the office . . ."

He let his words trail off when he sensed that Tech wasn't listening, then said, "Tech, what are you doing? Why aren't you exiting?"

Tech said nothing.

"Tech," Marz repeated.

"What's the green construct off to my left?" Tech asked.

"Environmental Protection Agency."

"Great! What d'you say we test-drive Subterfuge?"

"In the EPA?" Marz said in disbelief. In a warming world, short on energy resources, the EPA had become an agency of wide-ranging authority. "Excessive Punishment Assured, Tech. Their agents don't need warrants, and they don't believe in courts. We'd be safer test-driving Subterfuge in the FBI—"

"Come on, you want to see the soft in action as much as I do, and the EPA's the perfect place to try it out. Agency bloodhounds couldn't nab a bug if it bit 'em on the nose."

"And we're going to bite them how?"

"By deleting some of Felix's violations. He's gotta have a few backed up. Besides, that'll make up for the work we're not getting done."

"Dude, wouldn't it be easier just to get the work done?"

"Easier, but not nearly as much fun."

"Tech, I don't even know if I installed Subterfuge right."

"Am I talking to the right Marz Vega?"

Marz turned to the dentist's chair to glare at his gangly, visored brother. "Haven't we had enough close calls for one session?"

"Don't confuse the issue. This has nothing to do with thrills."

"Nothing to do with thrills, huh?"

"Open the garage again," Tech said, taking the Venom through a rapid turn. "We're going to need something a little less obvious than a racer."

The headquarters of the Environmental Protection Agency was a large, multiwindowed mushroom occupying an entire virtual block. Stacked at nearly every entry port were the myriad craft of telecommuting employees. Access to the construct, and indeed to most of the Network's vast cityscape of data domains, was typically restricted to staffers or privileged users with official clearance. But Tech and Marz's work for Felix McTurk had made them experts at cutting through security blankets.

Piloting an ancient biplane they'd nicknamed the Baron, Tech aimed himself for the least crowded entrance, the cyberflyer's virtual red scarf unfurling in the data breeze from the open cockpit.

True to its low-impact philosophy, there was nothing fancy about the EPA, either in decor or layout. Levels were color-coded according to the various departments to which they belonged, with narrow aisles wending between rows of file drawers. Once inside a drawer, you could move through the contents, open files, scan, edit, or download contents. If you had the appropriate codes, you could even delete items, in part or entirely.

You accomplished all this by using your joystick to click on whatever menu selections, option keys, or free-floating icons a site displayed, or by entering executable commands into your virtual keyboard.

Tech opened another song cache and began to familiarize himself with the construct's layout while Marz ran a search for Felix McTurk's file. Navigating bureaucratic quagmires like the EPA was exactly what Tech was paid to do, since Felix, despite his chosen profession, had little fondness for flying and a case of adult-onset claustrophobia when it came to negotiating bureaucratic corridors.

"I found Felix," Marz announced. "Level three, drawer 8504. That level's reserved for repeat offenders, so security's going to be thick."

"I'm on my way," Tech said, tweaking the joystick and depressing the accelerator pedal. The biplane banked to the right and sped off down a long green corridor.

Level three was even more heavily policed than he had expected it to be. But Tech managed to reach drawer 8504 without incident. Confident that Subterfuge would allow him to outsmart the EPA's watchdogs and trackers, he made a sharp turn into the drawer.

Even if the new software failed to do its job and a couple of security bloodhounds did pick up his scent, all would not be lost. To guard against just

such an eventuality—though not necessarily occurring at the EPA—Marz had patched Felix's cybersystem into the neural network computer that ran
the multinational insurance company in the office
next door to Data Discoveries. Any location trace
would stop at the insurance company's system.

With luck.

"Jeez! You should see this thing," Tech said
when he reached Felix's file. "Big as a cinder block
and pasted with overdue notices. Felix has been a
very bad boy."

"Play it safe," Marz cautioned. "Don't try to
delete too much."

"I want to give the hounds good reason to come
after me. Give the soft a real trial by fire."

Tech had just begun highlighting and deleting
some of Felix's more flagrant violations—the ones
resulting from energy misuse and failing to recy-
cle—when Marz's voice boomed through the headset earpieces.

"Heads up! The EPA has issued an intrusion
alert. Security programs are searching all levels for
undocumented arrivals."

Tech stopped what he was doing. "It's cool. I already deleted the worst of the violations. I'm heading out the drawer."

"Don't go out the way you came in. You've got
pit bulls and bloodhounds zeroing in on your position."

"Then it's time to bring out the big guns, bro.
Unzip Subterfuge."

Marz typed a flurry of commands on the keyboard. "Subterfuge is open," he said, crossing his fingers.

Tech glanced in the visor's rearview window in time to see a pack of shimmering, razor-toothed mastiffs come skittering around a turn in the corridor and race after him. His fingers danced over the joystick's control pad.

"Deploying ghosts."

Instantly, multiple images of the Baron took shape to all sides of him and began to veer off in different directions. All but one of the slavering mastiffs chased after the ghosts, and that one angled into the drawer Tech had just exited.

He hooted with joy.

"Subterfuge is awesome! No way those trackers will be able to pick out the real me!"

"Get yourself off level three just in case," Marz urged. "You're closest exit to the Ribbon is through the south gate on level one."

Tech rammed the joystick forward. The biplane veered and shot for the end of the corridor. But Tech wasn't halfway there when, out of nowhere, a program gremlin popped into existence and perched itself like a gargoyle on the Baron's upper-right wing tip. The product of free-floating data fragments, program gremlins were a fairly common sight in the Network. But this one was bright blue, from pointed ears to splayed feet and had a short tail, big black saucer-shaped eyes, and a yellow button nose.

"What the heck," Tech said. "This thing must have escaped from some gaming site."

Marz was already running diagnostic programs. "I'm not sure where it came from. It's made of some code I've never seen before. If I didn't know better, I'd swear it launched from Subterfuge."

Tech aimed the biplane's cockpit gun at the gremlin and sprayed it with a burst of minimizing code to no apparent effect. "Well, wherever it came from, I can't shake it loose! And it's getting *bigger*."

Marz stared at the monitor screen in mounting astonishment. "It's uploading data from the EPA's central-processing unit!" He hit the keyboard's record button, intent on downloading a backup file in case the office cybersystem crashed.

Tech slammed the joystick from side to side in an effort to dislodge the gremlin, which was continuing to swell as it gobbled data. The Baron's upper-right wing was already sagging under the weight of the cybercreature, and the biplane was in danger of stalling.

"Tech, get out of there!" Marz said. "The dogs are back on your scent. They're going to get a fix on us."

"The gremlin's slowing me down!" Tech yelled back. "I'm too heavy with code."

Marz nibbled at his left thumbnail while his right hand flew across the keyboard. "I found a closer exit. Go left at the next intersection and head straight down the corridor. The exit will be marked in red. Punch it!"

Tech's right foot depressed the accelerator pedal as far as it would go. Despite the presence of the now bloated gremlin, the retro plane managed to pick up a bit of speed as it negotiated the turn. Seconds later the exit came into view, growing larger and larger in the visor. Tech made a beeline for the irising portal. The Baron had almost reached it when an amorphous jet-black presence dropped from the arched ceiling, obscuring Tech's vantage on the exit and blotting out nearly all ambient light.

Tech worked the joystick and the foot pedals in a desperate attempt to find a path around the black curtain, but no matter where he moved, the thing kept positioning itself directly in front of him.

He was trapped.

Even with the accelerator floored, the Baron seemed to be hovering like a helicopter. It lurched once, but only to stall. Springing forward suddenly, the black mass draped itself over the plane like a collapsing parachute.

Fear began to gnaw at Tech's confidence.

What had he gotten himself into? He knew that he shouldn't be afraid, and yet he couldn't suppress a rising tide of panic. He wanted to lift the visor, but he couldn't bring himself to move. His heart thudded in his ears and against his ribs. He felt frozen inside.

Abruptly, a high-pitched, sharp voice that wasn't Marz's filled the headphones.

"That thing wants me, not you."

For a moment, Tech wasn't sure where the voice was coming from. Then he grasped that it was the voice of the saucer-eyed gremlin that had hitched itself to his craft.

"Huh? What?"

"Better let me handle this."

"Who are you?" Tech said. "*What* are you?"

"You just freed me."

"*I* freed you?"

"What'd you say?" Marz asked, swinging toward the dentist's chair in confusion.

"Follow my instructions," the gremlin told Tech. "If you hope to avoid falling into Scaum's clutches."

"Scaum?" Tech asked.

"The dark presence that is about to engulf you."

Tech swallowed hard and shoved the joystick to one side as wavering tentacles sprouting from the shadowy thing began to entwine his ship.

"You can't outrun it," the gremlin cautioned. "Surrendering control of your data craft to me is our only chance."

Marz heard Tech mumbling to himself. Again he swung away from the cybersystem console, this time to see Tech loosening his grip on the joystick and lifting his feet from the pedals.

"Tech, you're powering down! The EPA hounds are almost on top of you!"

Lowering the interface goggles he wore high on his forehead, Marz swiveled back to the console. One eye opened to the real world, the other gazing into cyberspace, he watched the Baron disappear into a utility shaft that wasn't indicated anywhere on the map of the EPA construct. Downloading all the information he could, Marz swiveled back to the dentist's chair, expecting to find Tech's hands back on the joystick. Instead they were raised to his shoulders.

"Tech, what the—"

Tech's right hand flashed a signal that he was all right, despite the plain fact that someone or something other than Tech was doing the flying.

Tech could imagine Marz's bewilderment, but he was in no position to put his brother at ease. The gremlin had dropped him into a bright-red shaft that bore a sickening resemblance to an artery, to the bottom of which Tech was now hurtling at incalculable speed. Close behind, the shadow—Scaum—was like crude oil racing through a pipeline, but losing distance with each passing nanosecond.

Tech wanted to say or do something, but he felt completely outside himself, a spectator to all that was occurring. The still unidentified gremlin had also fallen silent, but was continuing to demonstrate its mastery of cyberspace by taking the Baron through loops and rolls Tech wouldn't have thought possible. Then, all at once, he was out of the shaft and back on the grid, though so far from the Ribbon he might as well have been in the Wilds.

A glance at the rearview window revealed that the shadow was nowhere to be seen.

Marz's panicked voice shook him back to awareness.

"Tech, the EPA got a location trace on us! Data torpedoes incoming! We gotta log out!"

Tech glanced at the neon-blue gremlin, which gazed back at him.

"Thanks for the lift," the gremlin said.

With that, the bloated cybercreature detached itself from the wing and went streaking off toward the Wilds. Unburdened, the Baron soared to a higher level, handling like its old self once again. Tech powered the biplane through a long bank and made for the Ribbon.

With the Peerless Castle back in sight, he let his brother guide him to the nearest exit port. In a mere five seconds, the visor went from Network-active to transparent mode. The instant the visor cleared, Tech clamped his left hand around the lever that elevated the back of the dentist's chair and shot to his feet.

He wasn't a step from the chair when the cyber-system loosed a computerized *screeech,* and a storm of blue electricity began to gambol and cor-uscate across the stainless-steel console, which promptly buckled and belched a mushroom cloud of white smoke.

Chapter 4

WEB WARRIORS

Felix McTurk—slim, dark-haired, and slightly goofy-looking despite his thirty-four years—gave a sharp downward tug to the narrow lapels of his plaid sports jacket as he exited the elevator that had conveyed him to the sixty-fifth floor of the Empire State Building.

This was going to be the first day of his new life he promised himself as he strode with uncharacteristic confidence toward his office at the far end of the hallway. Things were going to take a turn for the better. No more worrying about his dwindling bank account, his confused love life, or the fact that the past decade hadn't turned out exactly as planned. In short, no more negative thinking. Work would pick up, he would pay off all his debts and outstanding violations, and good fortune would shine on him like never before.

Optimism alone was enough to paint

a broad smile on his face. But the smile began to
falter as he passed by the Sentinel Insurance
Agency, and from behind its heavy hardwood
doors came voices raised in dismay, along with a
smell of smoldering electronics.

Felix felt his stomach knot, but he quickly re-
gained his composure.

After all, what could Sentinel's woes have to do
with him?

His smile returned—though he did have to coax
it a bit.

The glass-paneled door to his office read: FELIX
MCTURK, DATA DISCOVERIES: MISSING PERSONS,
MISPLACED PROPERTY, DISAPPEARED INFORMA-
TION. He took hold of the doorknob, but didn't
turn it. Instead he cupped his left hand to his ear
and leaned against the pebbled-glass panel. Loud
humming and whirring noises greeted him, but he
heard none of the usual bass rumblings of Immor-
tal Riot or the frantic synthbeat of DJ Finger.

Relieved but still suspicious, Felix twisted the
knob and threw the door wide open. Tech was
seated at the largest of the office monitors, the
hood of his oversize sweatshirt raised and his
hazel-eyed gaze fixed intently on the display.
Diminutive Marz was across the room, his brown
hands buried in the innards of a processor case, installing some unidentifiable piece of hardware.

"Felix," they said in unison, loudly enough to be
heard over the noise of a portable air-conditioner
set on full blast and a quartet of ratcheting fans,
which were blowing strongly enough to whip

Felix's brimmed cap from his head, send it zipping around the office, and nearly out the open window.

Felix managed to snatch the cap in midflight. Then he glanced around. The console—which in most offices would have been a simple affair of processors, flat-screen monitors, and assorted input devices, but under Tech and Marz's charge had come to resemble a NASA technical station— looked conspicuously serene. No official interrupt-warning icons were pulsing from the screens, and Tech's headset sat neatly on the padded seat of the dentist's chair from which the kids accessed the Virtual Network.

"Why is it like winter in here?" Felix asked, pulling his jacket closed with one hand.

"Cool air makes you more productive," Tech said.

"Says who?"

"We heard it on the news," Marz explained, trading quick glances with Tech. "A special report."

"Then why's the window open? Or are we trying to make all of Manhattan more productive?"

"The report stressed just the right mix of cool and *fresh* air," Tech explained.

"Uh, huh," Felix said, planting his tongue in his cheek and nodding.

Casually he began to inch toward the wall switch that controlled the fans. The sight of Marz's widening eyes confirmed his suspicions. Tech saw what was coming and flew from his chair, hoping to reach the wall switch first, but Felix had the jump on him. No sooner did he throw the switch than wisps of acrid white smoke began to curl from beneath the edges of the console, two of the monitors, and one of the keyboards.

Felix's stomach sank. "Not again!"

"It wasn't our fault!" Marz said. "Not all of it, anyway."

Felix stared at him, slack-jawed. But before he could ask what it was this time that wasn't their fault, fists began to pound against the office door.

Felix whirled.

"Network Security," someone shouted from the hallway.

"Closed for lunch," Tech yelled. "Come back later."

The pounding continued, forceful enough to rattle the glass panel. "Open up, McTurk."

Marz had leaped from his chair and was suddenly at the office window. "Quick!" he said. "Building ledge to the window-washers' scaffold. I've seen it done in movies."

"Are you crazy?" Tech said. "That's the first place they'll look!"

"McTurk!" a second voice shouted from the hallway. "Don't force us to get a warrant."

"Yeah, force them to get a warrant," Tech said. "Force warrant! Force warrant!"

Felix glowered at him, then gestured silently for Marz to shut off the air-conditioner. When the machine's noisy compressor had wound down, Felix moved to the door and opened it.

A fire hydrant of a man shoved a badge in Felix's face as he stormed into the office followed by an equally stout woman. Both of them were dressed in the gray uniforms of Network Security—syscops.

The man put his stubby hands on his hips and ordered Felix to take a seat. Tech and Marz were edging toward the open door when the woman stepped in their path, blocking their exit.

"Hello, McTurk," the man began. "This is my partner, Sergeant Policks."

"Still walking the cyberbeat after all these years, Sergeant Caster?"

"That's *lieutenant*, McTurk." Caster slammed his hand against the air-conditioning unit. "You have a permit for this thing?"

"It's more like a piece of sculpture," Tech blurted, instantly regretting it when Felix scowled at him.

Policks sniffed in derision and glanced at the screen of a handheld computer. "This 'sculpture' has dropped the temperature in here to fifty-seven degrees, which is in clear violation of the Environmental Regulatory Act as it relates to the conspicuous consumption of energy."

"I'll get rid of the thing immediately," Felix said. "Tech, Marz, show this criminal device to the recycling bin." He forced himself to smile at the two syscops. "I'm also a big fan of clean air and drinkable water."

"Is that so?" Policks said. "Then how is it that you're continually being fined for recycling violations?"

"It's a conspiracy. Someone keeps mixing plastic bottles in with my regular trash."

"Save it, McTurk," Caster said. "You've got bigger problems than a couple of recycling violations." He approached Felix in a menacing way. "Earlier this morning, someone made an unauthorized Network run into the EPA's violations division."

Felix barely managed to keep from looking at Tech. "You're accusing me? On what grounds?"

Caster grinned nastily. "On the grounds that the only EPA file tampered with was *yours*."

"Oh," Felix said, blinking.

"The penetration was traced to the neural-net computer next door," Policks took over. "But once we took a closer look at the machine, what do you think we found?"

"That it hadn't been dusted in years?" Tech said.

Caster's round face flushed with anger. "We found an illegal timeshare patch, McTurk—a patch we have good reason to believe leads right here."

Felix feigned outrage. "Of all the—"

"Our records show that you've got a long history of questionable Network operations," Policks cut him off.

"Runs are part of my business," Felix said.

"And illegal runs are part of ours," Caster said.

"This lastest violation of Network space has put you over the top," Policks said. "As of immediately, you're shut down."

Felix shot to his feet. "You can't do that! How am I supposed to conduct business if I can't use my system? If you can't cut me some slack, do it for the boys."

Caster almost laughed. "Your long-term future's

not our concern, data dick. You've got twenty-four hours to settle up with Network Security *and* with the EPA. What's more, we catch you doing another illegal run, you'll be barred permanently from entering the Network."

Policks keyed a code into her handheld device, and not a moment later every monitor in the office was displaying a Network Security warning trefoil and a countdown timer.

While Felix was groaning, Caster let his stern gaze settle on Tech and Marz. "Why aren't you two in school?"

"Teachers conference," Marz said quickly.

"Snow day," Tech said at the same time.

The security man nodded dubiously, then he and his partner turned to go. Waiting in the hallway when they opened the door was a spindly woman with pinched features and dull-brown hair that curtained a narrow face. As if in defiance of the weather, she was wearing a turtleneck sweater and a wool skirt that fell nearly to her ankles.

"And who might you be?" Policks asked.

"Fidelia Temper," the woman said firmly, peering around Policks for a glimpse of the office. "I'm a counselor at the Safehaven group home on Fifty-sixth Street."

Caster jerked his thumb over his shoulder. "If you're looking for McTurk, he's inside. But I doubt he'll be here for much longer."

"That would suit me fine," Fidelia Temper said.

Policks showed her a twisted smile. "Your little hot-rodders are in there, too."

Fidelia shouldered between Policks and Caster

and stepped boldly into the office. Felix was sitting with his head in his hands.

"Mr. McTurk," she barked.

Felix glanced up at her, and his face fell even more. "Please, no flying monkeys," he muttered.

Muffled giggles came from the behind the closet door.

"Where are the boys, Mr. McTurk?" Fidelia said, her voice dripping with malice. She advanced a step and planted her hands on her hips. "Well?"

"Boys?"

Felix turned to where Tech and Marz had been sitting only moments earlier, then cut his gaze to the office closet. Frowning angrily, he walked across the room and pulled open the door, sending the two brothers tumbling to the carpet.

"You mean these boys? The ones who were supposed to be working on a case for me but decided instead to take a joy run into the EPA's Network construct?"

"You must have us mixed up with the other boys," Marz said.

"We were only trying to scarf some of your violations," Tech explained, getting to his feet.

"Well, nice going, *Jesse*," Felix said, using Tech's actual name. He gestured toward the cyberconsole. "Your help's not only brought the EPA down on my back, but Network Security, too."

"It was all my idea," Marz said, stepping forward.

Tech punched his brother gently on the arm and gave him a "no way" look.

Fidelia Temper scowled at Felix. "I know you think you're helping Jesse and Marshall by employing them here. But I will not tolerate your doing that at the expense of their education."

When neither Tech nor Marz would meet his gaze, Felix looked at Fidelia. "No teachers conference? No snow day?"

She shook her head. "I want them back in school this moment!" She turned and stamped out of the office.

Felix shot Tech and Marz a withering look. "When are you two going to wise up?"

"Tomorrow," Tech said, offering a Scout's honor salute.

Felix compressed his lips. "Not soon enough. You're not flying for me anymore."

Tech's jaw dropped. "Felix, you don't mean that. You need us. You don't even *like* to fly."

"That's beside the point," Felix said, waving his arms about. "Look at this mess. I'm ruined!"

"We can have the system back up and running in no time," Marz said.

"What, so you can make another illegal run into the Motor Vehicle Bureau or somewhere?" He studied them for a moment. "How'd you get past EPA security, anyway?"

"You don't want to know," Tech said.

"New software we got from the Warehouse," Marz said sheepishly.

Felix held his hands to his ears. "I don't want to know."

"Told ya," Tech said.

"Felix," Marz said with sudden enthusiasm. "Something bizarre happened on the run. First, this program gremlin landed on the Baron's wing."

"Even Marz didn't see it coming," Tech added.

"Then this shadowy thing called Scaum appeared out of nowhere—"

"Not out of nowhere," Felix interrupted. "You were breaking into the EPA. What did you expect security to do, announce itself with balloons and fireworks?"

"Nuh-uh," Tech said. "The EPA uses standard-issue security hounds. Now, all of a sudden, it's deploying security shadows? Besides which, Scaum wasn't like any security sentinel I've ever been up against. In fact, I'm not even sure it was a program."

"Behaved more like a neural net," Marz said, nodding.

"But the weird thing is that the gremlin saved me from Scaum. And that isn't even the half of it. I was—"

"Enough!" Felix said, holding up his hands.

"But, Felix, the gremlin said I *freed* it. What if it was kidnapped?"

Felix stared at Tech in theatrical disbelief. "You're listening to some reject game-world gremlin now?"

"I'm not saying I believe it," Tech said. "It was all happening so fast . . ." He turned to Marz. "Play him the download, bro."

Marz took his lower lip between his teeth and shook his head. "We lost it when the system crashed."

Tech blew out his breath in exasperation, then swung back to Felix. "The gremlin even thanked me."

"Good," Felix said. "Then case closed."

"But—"

Felix held up his hands again. "Listen to me— both of you. I've warned you about wasting what little I pay you on street software. Those programs never work as promised. And I'm a data dick not a police detective, which means I don't do kidnappings."

Tech pointed to the glass panel in the office door. "The sign says 'missing persons.' "

"*Persons,*" Felix stressed, "not gremlins. Can't you stay in the real world for a change?"

Tech averted Felix's gaze. "The gremlin and the shadow were real, Felix."

"Just like the rest of your Network legends, Jess. And no more skipping school, understand?"

Felix watched the boys hang their heads. He was hardly a good role model for them, but the least he could do was try to sound like an adult.

"Now, get going."

Glumly, Tech spun on his heel and headed for the door with Marz only a step behind.

Chapter 5

WEB WARRIORS

The Safehaven group home for "transitional teens" occupied the lower three floors of an old hotel. Tech sat on his unmade bed in the cramped room he shared with his brother, notebook computer opened in his lap, trying to wrap his attention around the homework he had failed to turn in along with the extra assignments his teachers had given him as punishment for missing class. For the past ten minutes, he had been staring blankly at the one sentence he had managed to write for an essay that was required to be no less than ten pages long and due no later than the following morning.

He couldn't get his mind off what had happened during the run into the EPA, which, in recollection, seemed more like a half-recalled bad dream. Felix was probably right—it was ridiculous to put any stock in the mad mutterings of a program gremlin—but Tech couldn't dismiss it so easily.

Where had the blue gremlin come from? From the ghost program, Subterfuge, as Marshall suspected or from somewhere in the EPA? And what sort of EPA data had it gorged itself on?

Then there was Scaum, the shapeless shadow that had gone after the gremlin—and Tech in the process. The dismal thing hadn't responded like a security program, so what was it, and what did it want with the gremlin? And finally there was the way the gremlin had piloted the Baron almost clear across the grid, executing precision maneuvers Tech rarely witnessed outside of computer-generated simulations.

It was like the Network rules had changed overnight.

He wanted to know what the gremlin had meant by saying that Tech had freed it, and he wanted to know where it had gone after it had abandoned the Baron's upper wing and fled toward the Wilds. But with the corruption of the backup file, it was all a wash. Just another Network mystery—or "legend," as Felix put it.

Network legends abounded. There was, for instance, the one about the hacker who, little by little, had been taken over by the programs he wrote; all make and manner of gremlins and ghosts, gifted with extraordinary powers, and escaped from games or born in the fathomless canyons of the Virtual Network itself; and Area X, a site buried deep in the Wilds where rumored First Contact had been made with aliens . . .

Tech loosed a despondent sigh.

He'd lost a race to Bios7, Felix was angry at him,

and Fidelia Temper was threatening to suspend his weekend privileges if he cut school again.

Life didn't always suck, but it sucked just now.

He set the notebook aside and gazed around the room at the mishmash of computer hardware, sports gear, old books, music synthesizers, and assorted pieces of thrift-store clothing that reflected his and Marz's few interests, as well as their general disregard for order. Untidiness was not uncommon in the group home, but the seeming deliberateness behind the mess in the Vega brothers' room singled it out from those of their home mates and had made them the bane of counselor Fidelia Temper's existence.

They had resided in the home for four years now, after a six-year stay with a great-aunt in upstate New York. Their aunt had taken them in after their parents had died in the crash of their private plane somewhere in the South Pacific. The aunt, too, had been a world traveler, and the fact that she spent more time in faraway places than she did at home was what had led to Tech and Marz's eventual enrollment in Safehaven, where it was believed that they could be better supervised. Everyone involved in their relocation had been convinced that the brothers' repeated school absences and minor troublemaking were due to the fact that they'd grown up with too much freedom. But, in fact—and much to the continuing dismay of Safehaven's director and councilors—Tech and Marz's penchant for skirting the rules had only increased since the move to New York City.

It wasn't that they hated school or were inca-

pable of learning. They simply had a difficult time
adjusting to the drudgery of homework and the
narrow-mindedness of certain schoolmates who
refused to accept that Tech and Marz were, well,
different.

For as long as he could remember, Tech had always had trouble staying seated at a desk, raising
his hand before answering questions, or caring
much about spelling and basic math skills—since
even the simplest computers had spellcheck and
calculator functions, and Tech couldn't ever pic-
ture himself being without a computer. But he
wasn't a cybergeek. He thought of computers as
vehicles, no different from snowboards, 'blades, or
mountain bikes when you got right down to it.
Computers provided him with a means of reaching
the edge and riding that edge for all it was worth.

For Tech, cyberflying was an extreme sport—the
extremest of sports.

Marz, by contrast, had been a worry to any
number of teachers and guidance councilors precisely because of too much sitting—in front of
screens of one sort or another, music synthesizers,
or with books far more advanced than those being
read by his age group. He took little interest in
sports or social activities, but when it came to de-
signing and customizing cybercraft, there were few
that could touch him.

Short and dark-complexioned, with a headful of
brown curls and eyes like mood rings, Marz was
contemplative and self-possessed, while loose-
limbed, blond-haired Tech was dismissive and
quick to anger.

When they were young, the fact that their aunt had elected to dress them in items she brought back from remote areas of the world rather than in the latest mall fashions further distanced the brothers from their classmates and had often made them objects of ridicule or worse. Tech had been able to handle whatever anyone dished out, but the razzing had been hard on Marz, and Marz's sensitivity had turned Tech into a fighter.

Tech never looked for fights. But anyone who messed with Marz could count on quick retaliation from his older brother.

So they had made the most of their aunt's travels and the gullibility of the caretakers in whose charge she left them to avoid school as often as possible, bonding as only brothers could even in pursuit of their separate obsessions. Relocated to New York City and placed suddenly under the supervision of strict disciplinarians like Fidelia Temper, they had been forced to find more creative ways to skip school. But, as before, they could invariably be found exploring the infinite realms of the Virtual Network, the one interest they shared.

Tech and Marz weren't the first kids of their generation to realize that the world they had been born into had been mapped to the square inch from space and largely drained of real-life adventure. Tropical forests of the sort Tarzan had swung through and that had once concealed the cities of vanished civilizations had all but disappeared, and with them had gone countless species of spectacular animals. Advances in satellite telecommunication had made it possible to make and receive phone calls from anywhere on the globe. Similarly, locators—worn on wrist or belt or implanted beneath the skin—had made it all but inconceivable that one would ever become lost, kidnapped, taken hostage, or grabbed by an angry parent and spirited off to Pakistan or Patagonia.

Privacy had been surrendered for safety.

Daredevils and reality-show contestants had replaced explorers.

And more troubling to Tech, movies, TV, music, and computer games had been made tame, except for the stuff being turned out by rebellious artists headquartered in the Wilds of the Network. Attempts were even being made to housebreak the final frontier—cyberspace—by monitoring the movements of frequent flyers and installing filters and security booths at nearly every entry port and grid intersection.

The only upside of all this was that the world had become dependent on technology, and the more you knew about computers, digicams, and bar codes, the easier it was to circumvent all the rules and regulations. In the Network, Tech and Marz had discovered all the adventure they had sought in vain in the real world—domains almost beyond their dreams, sites catering to every thinkable fantasy, and a vast underground community of hackers and cyberjockeys, entry into which didn't depend on age, gender, how fashionably you dressed, or how skilled you were at playing ball.

Two years earlier they had responded to an on-Network help-wanted ad directed at cyberjocks with a talent for finding missing data. The ad had been placed by Felix McTurk, an adept and one-time successful data detective who had found himself falling behind the technological curve, mainly because of his fear of cyberflying. Felix had given the brothers a series of tests, which they had aced, and—sight unseen—had ultimately offered them jobs. When he realized that he had hired two teenagers, however, Felix had withdrawn the offer. But he had been so impressed by Tech and Marz's skills, he had started giving them occasional assignments. Before too long they were spending more time at Data Discoveries than they were at school or at the group home.

Felix was well meaning but he just didn't understand life on the edge. He saw Marz as a budding cyberarchitect, and Tech as an executive data manager. But Tech wanted more from his future than the promise of steady money. He craved excitement. Felix was in danger of becoming one of those people who settled into a groove as they aged, and Tech was determined to help him avoid that fate—without sabotaging Data Discoveries in the process—if he could manage it.

When Tech realized that his thoughts had begun to trail off into daydreams, he retrieved the notebook and woke it up. He was halfway into a second sentence for the essay when Fidelia Temper's shrill voice found its way through the room's closed door.

"And another thing," the group home counselor was saying, "there'll be no more TV time in the common room until you demonstrate to me that you can pick up after yourself and lend a hand around here for a change."

Marz rapped a code on the door and Tech told him to come in.

Marz gave him a secret smile as he entered. Most of Fidelia remained in the hall, but she craned her thin neck through the doorway far enough to direct a suspicious look at Tech.

"Working on your extra assignments, Jesse?" she asked, fairly basking in the question.

He peered at her over the laptop's screen. "I live for homework."

She ignored the remark and glanced around the room in dismay. "You know, we used to have a name for places like this."

"Power spots," Tech said.

"Mad-scientist laboratories," Marz chimed in.

"Pig sties!" Fidelia said with high-pitched indignation. "And let me tell you something. If you care at all about your futures, you'll stay as far away from that data detective as you can get."

"Better a dead end with Felix than a future with the Bride of Frankenstein," Tech muttered.

Fidelia opened her mouth to reply, but words evidently failed her, and she slammed the door.

Tech frowned, but Marz's smile only broadened.

"Marz . . ." Tech said quietly. "I know that look. Spill it."

Marz fished a minidisk from the breast pocket of his T-shirt and held it between his thumb and forefinger. "The backup file of the EPA run. I managed to reconstruct some of it."

Tech leaped off the bed. "You rule! Let me see!"

Marz coin-flipped the mini to Tech, who imme-diately slotted the disk into the laptop.

"Man, you shoulda seen what I had to go through to decode even part of it," Marz boasted.

His eyes glued to the laptop screen, Tech could barely contain his excitement. "You are a friggin' gen-ee-us!" An alphanumeric jumble began to scroll on the screen, then the image of the blue gremlin appeared, and its high-pitched, youthfully eager voice issued from the computer's small speakers, repeating in a loop.

"MSTRNTS. MSTRNTS will know what to do."

Tech highlighted the short run of capitalized text that accompanied the image in a dialogue balloon and copied it to a separate file. When it was clear that the remainder of the download contained nothing more than indecipherable code, Tech opened the text file and studied the words.

"What's a 'MSTRNTS'?"

"Could be a she," Marz said.

"A she?"

Marz reached over Tech's shoulder, moved the cursor, unlocked the caps key, and inserted a pe-riod and space. "Ms. Trents. See?"

Tech laughed through his nose. "Like the letters on a vanity license plate."

"Might even be a vanity plate."

Tech considered it briefly. "Then why not Ms. Trants, or Ms. Tronts. Or even Ms. T. Rents?"

"Okay," Marz conceded. "But those still make her a she."

"Not necessarily," Tech said, typing. "If it's like a vanity tag, then maybe m-s-t-r is short for 'mister.' "

Marz plucked his lower lip. "Mr. Nats, Nets . . ."

"Nits, Nots," Tech completed. "Could be any one of them, or something completely different. Maybe there's another hint in the download. We could run it through Codebreaker, or we could bring the mini to one of the cypherpunks downtown."

"We could," Marz said slowly, "but I think our little blue gremlin is already telling us what to do: Bring it to 'MSTRNTS.' "

They stared at the letters for a long while.

"Ms. Tree Nuts?" they asked each other at the same time. Tech punched Marz in the arm and broke out laughing.

As long as they were together, life didn't suck.

Felix sat staring at the flashing countdown icon he had moved to the corner of the office's main-display screen—the only screen that was still working. Felix had exactly sixteen hours ten minutes to settle up with Network Security and the EPA, or Data Discoveries would be history.

"How much money do I owe in fines?" he asked the computer.

"$28,865," the system replied in an electronic monotone.

"Twenty-eight thousand?" Felix mumbled in disbelief.

Most of that amount was in interest, springing

from unpaid vehicular emission-control and
garbage-recycling violations. He refused to even
think about his soon-to-be-overdue rent and insurance payments.

"How much is in the account?" he asked at last.
"$301.27."

Hopeless, Felix thought. He supposed he could
throw himself on the mercy of the court and plead
for a week's extension, but what good would a
week do?

He was angry with Jess and Marshall for adding
to his financial woes, but he couldn't blame them
entirely. He was the one who had allowed the fines
to pile up and compound. The boys had deserved
the dressing down they had received, but Felix already missed them and feared being estranged
from them even more than being put out of business.

He let go a prolonged exhale that marked an official end to the day that was supposed to have
been the first day of his new life. Then he activated
the office answering machine, which told him that
he had had three calls—better than three times the
usual number, zero.

All three were routine requests from people who
had fallen prey to the complexity of modern life.
One woman's money-market funds had disappeared overnight. The bank claimed to have an
e-authorization for withdrawal, but the woman
claimed that she had sent no such authorization. A
second woman had purchased a round-trip travel
package to Tibet only to end up incarcerated in the

capital city for not being able to show a prebooked return flight. A father of three was looking for his eldest son who had left home with all of dad's ATM and credit cards.

He rubbed his eyes as he regarded the screen. None of the cases would pay much, but they would at least help cover the fines.

Precisely at 8:00 P.M. the private videophone line intruded with a series of tones. The caller obviously had access to Felix's personal number, so odds were in favor of the call being legitimate and not an attempt to get him to switch his long-distance service or donate to Casualties of the Stock-Market Crash.

"42212-667-6766," Felix said, picking up at last.

"Felix McTurk?"

Felix waited. The phone's video-display screen remained blank. "That depends on who's calling."

"A prospective client, Mr. McTurk."

To Felix's trained ear, the caller was a kid making use of a voice processor to sound older. There was, however, a trace of an accent he couldn't identify.

"You mind telling me who gave you this number, Mr. . . ."

"Gitana," the voice told him. "Magyar Gitana. And I'd rather not reveal the source, Mr. McTurk."

"Is this a data case, Mr. Gitana?"

"I need help with the transferal of some sensitive information. The run will have minimal environmental impact."

Felix directed a puzzled frown at the phone. "Environmental impact?"

"Would you be willing to fly for me, Mr. McTurk? It's what you do best, isn't it?"

"Well, I'm as good as most and better than some," Felix lied. "The problem is, my cybersystem is, uh, temporarily out of commission while it undergoes an upgrade."

"For our purposes, it would be best if you did *not* fly from your personal system."

"Back up a second," Felix said. "You've got the wrong number if you're planning an illegal run. Just how sensitive is this information you want transferred?"

"Its value to me is incalculable. I have reason to believe that certain outside agencies are also eager to lay hands on it."

Felix jotted notes on an electronic pad. "Are we talking about federal agencies or private ones?"

Gitana fell silent briefly. "Maybe both."

Felix shook his head in impatience. "We're getting nowhere fast. How do you figure I can help you if I don't have access to a cybersystem?"

"I've already taken the liberty of signing you up for an introductory tour of the Network sponsored by Virtual Horizons on Broadway near Thirty-third Street."

"I'm listening."

"Be there for the ten A.M. tour and I'll meet you inside the Network at precisely ten-fifteen. At that time, I will furnish you with additional information regarding the data I wish retrieved, along with instructions for redepositing them."

"Frankly, I don't like the sound of this."

"My sources tells me that you once had a thriving business, Mr. McTurk. I can put you back on the fast track. Call up your bank records."

"What?"

"Humor me. It will benefit you greatly."

Felix called his bank records on-screen. One moment there was $301.27 in the account, and the next there was $29,301.27—enough to cover almost all his debts. He stared at the figure in disbelief.

"The adjusted amount will remain, whether or not we succeed in our mission. Should we succeed, you can expect an additional fifteen thousand dollars by no later than three o'clock tomorrow afternoon."

Felix was already calculating how he would spend the extra bucks. "One thing," he said after a moment. "Let's suppose the Network meet doesn't go as planned. How do I get in touch with you?"

"You don't," Gitana said with a note of finality.

Tech and Marz gazed groggily at the glowing display of the laptop. Neglecting homework assignments and dinner, they had spent the entire evening attempting to discover the identity of "MSTRNTS," and their efforts had left them screen-weary. They had performed Network searches on dozens of names and possible words, and on hundreds of permutations of those same names and words. None, however, had furnished any conspicuous links with the gremlin that had emerged from Subterfuge or from the EPA.

Yawning loudly, Tech ordered their favorite search engine to see what it could do with the words "mystery notes," which Marz had come up with while doodling in the margin of a sheet of homework.

The laptop emitted a chorus of chirps and text filled the screen.

" 'Musical notes that once emerged mysteriously on analog and other low-tech recordings,' " Tech read aloud. "A music store in Philadelphia, another in Phoenix. A specialty bookstore in London . . . yada, yada."

He scrolled down, then suddenly stopped and sat back in plain surprise.

"What is it?" Marz asked, leaning over Tech's shoulder for a better look at the screen.

"Harwood Strange."

Marz's brow furrowed. "I know that name from somewhere . . ."

Tech tasked the laptop to conduct a search on Harwood Strange. "A hacker from last decade," Tech said as he perused the data. "Became a kind of recluse after a hack that went bad—*real* bad. Some run that threatened national security or something."

"Wait a minute," Marz said. Pivoting the laptop toward him, he did rapid input at the keyboard. "Harwood Strange wasn't just any hacker. He wrote *The Strange Manifesto*—his vision of the Network as free cyberspace without filters or speed traps. He was a visionary, man, a real eccentric."

Marz tapped the screen with his forefinger as additional text appeared. "Harwood Strange was a musician."

"Yeah, and . . . ?"

Marz turned to his brother. "*Mystery Notes* was the title of his most famous DVD."

Chapter 6

WEB WARRIORS

"Mr. McTurk, we're thrilled that you have chosen Virtual Horizons to introduce you to the wonders of the Network," Virtual Horizons' tour guide, Ms. Dak, said when Felix showed up for the tour his mystery client had booked for him. "Have you ever flown before?"

"Only the friendly skies."

"Friendly skies?"

"An old advertising slogan," Felix explained. "Before your time, I guess."

Dak smiled. "Well, I'm certain I would have laughed if I had understood the reference."

Felix suddenly felt old. He figured Dak for about twenty-one. With her perfect teeth, bottle tan, muscles shaped by machines, and form-hugging clothes, she was typical of the new executive class. As fresh and bright as the new century itself.

"Is this tour for business or pleasure?" she asked.

"Pure pleasure," Felix said.

She escorted him into a waiting area filled with other tourists, many of them actual tourists visiting New York City—some thirty people from obscure nation states in Asia, Africa, and the Middle East where accessing the Virtual Network was still a dream.

Felix handed over a credit card and submitted to a face-recognition scan. Then a technician not much older than Tech showed him to an interface recliner that was a much more padded affair than Data Discoveries' refurbished dentist's chair. Once seated he was fitted with a visor, earbeads, and a motion-capture vest and introduced to the basics of operating the multibutton joystick and the foot pedals. The technician explained that while most of the initial piloting would be done by Virtual Horizons, there would a short period at the conclusion of the tour where everyone would spend ten minutes sampling some of the immersive thrill rides offered by Grand Adventure.

Felix noticed straight away that the motion-capture vest was dialed down to the lowest setting, since it wasn't uncommon for novice flyers to experience vertigo and mild nausea.

Regardless, his palms were already damp with sweat.

He nodded to the tourists seated in the chairs to either side of him as a sweet-smelling female attendant with a delicate touch ran a quick test of the interface wardrobe and hookups. Additional instructions were given through the earbeads and de-

livered in the carefully modulated voice actual
flight attendants employed.

"In the event of an emergency exit . . ."

Felix was so accustomed to Jess and Marshall's
casual attitude toward cyberflying that the tour
suddenly struck him as novel and daring. No
sooner had Ms. Dak and the young technician
donned their wardrobes than Felix's visor went
from transparent to Network-active mode, and the
virtual ecology—the unreal estate—of the Network began to take shape before his eyes, making
him feel as if he were gliding above a glowing, mul-
tileveled cityscape of gargantuan domes, pyramids,
spheres, and towers rising up into an impossibly
blue sky.

A few of the other flyers gasped in astonishment.

A wave of dizziness overcame Felix, and a rivulet
of sweat took a bumpy ride down along his ribs.
He hadn't always been a fearful flyer. But then, the
Network hadn't always been quite so *real*.

Cybervehicles of all description were moving
along the grid's busy thoroughfares and crosslinks.
Though most of the vehicles were mass-produced
craft resembling ultralight gliders, jet planes, SUVs
and sports cars, every so often a custom craft
would flash into view, exuberant with strobing
lights, spotted as a jungle cat, or designed to con-
vey some sense of the craft's pilot.

Felix wasn't surprised to find that the bus he and
the rest of Virtual Horizons' tourists were flying
was adorned with advertisements for the company
itself.

The slogan read, VIRTUAL HORIZONS—OPEN YOUR EYES TO A BETTER REALITY!

The mellifluous voice of Ms. Dak drifted through the headset earbeads over a subdued soundtrack of cloying music.

"Welcome to the world of cyberspace," she began, "and the adventure of a lifetime. Some of you might be feeling a bit dizzy at the moment, but the feeling will pass shortly. Just sit back, relax, and leave the piloting to us."

Felix took her at her word and settled back into the comfy flight chair.

This isn't so bad, he told himself. He could handle this.

"If you look to the left you can see the spire of the CiscoSoft Telecomputer Construct," Dak continued. "And off to the right as we continue our slow spiral down toward the heart of the grid stands the landmark IBM storage facility. The cityscape of constructs along the eastern horizon belongs to Mitsuni, and the enormous medieval castle in the distance is the headquarters of Peerless Engineering, which created much of what you're seeing."

Felix took a long calming breath. The descent was smoother than any Jess or Marshall had ever taken him through. He sensed that he was in the hands of a veteran pilot. Because piloting was by and large a function of state-of-mind, it said a lot about a cyberjockey when he or she could keep the ride unruffled and the maneuvers to a minimum. Virtual Horizons wasn't in the business of providing the kind of thrills you could get in the arcades, in any case.

The tour was closing on InfoWorld when Felix began to experience a subtle change. By degrees his virtual seat was dropping behind the rest of the group, and the ride was becoming jerky. A glance at the visor's time display confirmed his suspicions: Magyar Gitana was inside the Network and trying to assume remote control of him.

Without warning he felt himself being sucked into a headlong dive parallel to the banner-plastered cliff face of InfoWorld. Despite his best effort to remain calm, a protracted *ahhhh!* tore from his mouth and his sweaty hands tightened on the padded arms of the flight chair.

Within seconds he was being propelled at high speed down the Ribbon, then powered through sudden turns, rocketed across canyons, spiraled through windows and insertion points, and finally shot toward the stylish headquarters of Worldwide Cellular.

His stomach heaved, and an acidic taste back-washed into his throat.

Then the accented, falsely deep voice of his client whispered through the earbeads.

"I'm so glad to see you, Mr. McTurk," Gitana said with adolescent enthusiasm. "Please remember to remain aware of where you are in the real world, and refrain from further outbursts of excitement."

That wasn't *excitement,* Felix wanted to tell him, that was panic! But he managed to keep silent.

"We'll be entering Worldwide Cellular," Gitana

went on. "Once inside, I'm going to steer you to the data I want you to retrieve, which are nested close to Cellular's switching nucleus."

Felix cursed to himself. Gitana hadn't said anything about pulling off an infiltration run.

"Perhaps you're thinking that this constitutes theft. But I assure you that the data bundle belongs to me, and that I'm doing no more for myself than what you do for your clients. As to why I'm not making the retrieval myself, let me say simply that, at present, I lack the resources."

Felix barely kept from speaking out loud.

"I'm aware that Virtual Horizons' joystick doesn't allow you to perform a fraction of the tasks you can perform through your office cyber-system," Gitana went on. "But even its limited abilities will allow us to accomplish our goal. Flick your joystick to the right if you understand all that I'm telling you, and so I can see that I have full control."

Felix did as Gitana requested.

"Good," his client said. "Once I've steered you into the switching nucleus, use your controller to highlight and drag the data I indicate. You may find it a bit cumbersome, as we're going to be uploading several terabytes of information. We're going to insert the dragged package into a cellular call I will place at the appropriate moment. Is that clear?"

Felix nudged the joystick.

Gitana proceeded to foil Cellular's security programs by deploying chaff clouds, program dazzlers, and logic bombs from a seemingly limitless arsenal of espionage weaponry. Confronted with this, Felix felt useless. But the more he studied the route Gitana was laying out, the more he saw room for improvement. He used the joystick to plot what he thought might constitute a safer path.

"Yes," Gitana said. "I see what you're getting at."

The course of Felix's liberated bus seat was adjusted. He began to feel his heart race as Gitana guided the pod deeper into the virtual construct, straight into Cellular's core. An entry port blinked open, and the visor showed a color-coded vista of converging cell-phone calls and pager transmissions resembling tracer rounds fired from ground-based artillery.

Then they were inside the nucleus and tearing along the route Felix had helped to plot, cloaked from infiltration filters arrayed like suspension bridges across immeasurably deep canyons.

Gitana indicated a neatly wrapped but enormous parcel of data concealed among the millions of calls. Felix feared that dragging the data could affect the entire operation of Worldwide Cellular. Trusting that Gitana had considered the repercussions, he clicked and dragged the data from its nesting place.

Immediately Gitana launched Felix from the core into the operating system and presumably toward the call to which Felix was supposed to affix the pilfered terabytes. The trajectory took him through a web of phone calls, surely disrupting service to tens of thousands of cell-phone users. Felix couldn't imagine what the massive data bundle contained, but he scarcely had time to think about it before security programs designed to resemble giant steel-jawed wire cutters poured from the tap Gitana had sunk into the switching nucleus and hastened after him.

Felix stifled an alarmed outburst and began to flick his joystick incessantly.

"Change of plan," Gitana said, after what seemed an eternity. "We'll have to deliver the data in person. Hang on, Mr. McTurk."

Boosted from Cellular with extraordinary velocity, Felix gave silent thanks to Virtual Horizons' flight attendant for having damped down the motion-capture vest. With the security cutters still in close pursuit, Gitana launched him breathtakingly high above Cellular, then sent him streaking across the grid like a meteor. Felix watched the Ribbon, the Peerless Castle, and the dreaded Escarpment disappear below him, and all at once found himself free-falling toward a nondescript eight-sided construct located in the Wilds of the Network.

"Drop the data bundle into the octagon," Gitana said without his usual calm. "Drop it now! Hurry!"

Harwood Strange was widely profiled on the Network, but if he had an e-address or a phone number, they were either unregistered or listed under a different name. Stumped, Tech and Marz had set about locating and downloading a copy of Strange's *Mystery Notes* DVD-ROM. Fleetingly popular a decade earlier, the self-published interac-

tive album featured track after track of extraordinary music, each composition linked to various
Network sites. Contact information provided with
the album had given the brothers a starting point
for tracing Strange's current whereabouts.

On learning that he lived in eastern Long Island,
only an hour's monorail ride from the group home,
they had decided to pay him a personal visit.

School would have to wait.

The town was small and weather-beaten, the
shingled homes bleached gray by the nearby ocean.
From the elevated monorail, Tech and Marz had
gotten glimpses of working farms, fruit stands,
vineyards, and fishing boats returning with fresh
catch. The first hint of spring was visible in the
green lawns that fronted enchanting homes. Surveillance cameras were obvious at the monorail
station, but scarce in the town itself. Painted signs
posted in the central square warned against loiter-
ing, boarding, 'blading, and noise. A plastic playground sat inside a circle of cushioning material.

Strange's address corresponded to an apartment
over a bait store in sore need of renovation. A
creaky, dilapidated exterior staircase ended at a
door stripped bare by wind and salt spray. The
boys picked their way to the top and, after a moment of hesitation, knocked.

The man who eventually answered was a
stooped giant with long, unruly gray hair and a
thick beard. He was wearing a hooded cloth
bathrobe that was spattered with either different
colors of paint or various foodstuffs—egg yellow,
strawberry red, coffee brown, jalapeño green. He

gave his head a sudden tilt that slid wire-rimmed glasses to the tip of his long nose, and he looked Tech and Marz up and down.

"The lawn doesn't need mowing and the windows don't need washing."

The boys traded glances. "We don't do that kind of work," Marz said.

"Well, you should think about doing it. You can make good money." His gray eyes narrowed behind the rectangular lenses of his glasses. "Don't tell me you're selling cookies."

"We're not selling anything or collecting for anything," Tech said.

"Then I can only assume that you're lost."

"Not even—if this is 466 Maple," Marz told him.

The man twisted around to regard the rusted numbers nailed above the door, then eyed the brothers once more while he scratched at his beard.

"Are you Mystery Notes?" Tech asked.

The man's eyes widened, and a short laugh escaped him. "Ah, right to the point, I see."

"I'm Tech. This is my brother, Marz."

Strange squinted at them, scrutinizing Tech's blond hair and Marz's nut-brown face and curly dark hair. "You two are brothers?"

Tech gave his standard reply. "We were designed to be different."

"Tech and Marz?" Strange said skeptically. "Those sound like robot names. And yet you appear to be flesh and blood."

"We're cyberflyers," Marz said, staring at

Strange as if he were a comic superhero come to life. "Tech and Marz are our user names."

" 'Robots in disguise,' " Strange sang, then straightened somewhat and rubbed his bearded chin. "What exactly brought you to my humble abode, Tech and Marz?"

Marz held up the minidisk. "This."

Strange took the disk between his thumb and forefinger and peered at it curiously.

"Most of the data is encrypted," Tech said, "except for one phrase. The phrase says that Mystery Notes will know what to do."

Strange's eyes darted from the disk to Tech. "Who's doing the talking?"

"We're hoping you can tell us," Tech said. "Do you believe in Network legends?"

"Legends of what sort?" Strange inquired, his eyes sparkling. "Spooks? Spies? Aliens? Mad, gray-haired hackers?"

"Ghosts in the machine," Tech said. "Program gremlins, in this case. A gremlin that knows you."

"A . . . program gremlin actually mentions me by name—Mystery Notes?"

"Actually, what it says is 'm-s-t-r-n-t-s.' " Marz explained.

"We ran hundreds of possible combinations," Tech said. "Mystery Notes was the only phrase that made sense because of the link to you."

"Then you know who I am."

"Author of *The Strange Manifesto*," Tech said.

"Legendary cyberflyer," Marshall added almost breathlessly. "Freeware radical. Musical genius. *Mystery Notes* is awesome sound."

"Well, I can see that you boys have good taste."
Strange sniffed in playful derision and stepped
back from the door. "Come in."

The tiny, two-room apartment was crawling
with cats, many of whom came running to rub
themselves against Tech's and Marz's legs. The
shabby, cat fur–covered furniture and woven rugs
looked as if they had come from great distances
and been made by people who lived in a different
century. The place was also filled with instruments
of endless variety—reed, stringed, keyed, and
skinned. Obsolete computer processors, boxy
monitors, peculiar keyboards, and laser printers
took up an entire wall. Elsewhere were piles of
hardcover books, graphic novels, videotapes, CDs,
minidiscs, and DVDs—libraries of information
that were now accessible with a few quick key-
strokes or could be amassed electronically in individual rental-storage facilities in the Network.

Strange planted himself in a padded swivel chair
before a large, dust-covered monitor and slipped
the minidisk into an ancient reader that lacked a
cover. For a long moment, he studied the jumble of
numbers and letters that resolved on-screen, then
he sat back, tugging on his beard.

"I know this code," he said at last, poising his
crooked fingers over the keyboard. "Let's see if we
can't get this critter to tell us in plain speak what
it's after."

Strange's fingers began to fly across the keys, all
of which were apparently linked to a music syn-
thesizer, so that each phrase of input constituted a
musical composition. He crossed his hands over

one another and expanded his reach to cover the
entire keyboard. When he struck the enter key for
the final time he might as well have been playing
the last chord of a piece of classical music.
Throwing his hands up, he leaned back from the
keyboard like a piano virtuoso waiting for applause—which Marz, unable to contain his excitement, provided.

An instant later, the voice of the program gremlin issued through the room's untold number of
speakers.

"My name is Cyrus Bulkroad," the gremlin
began. "I'm trapped, MSTRNTS. I need your
help."

Strange didn't say anything for a long while. He
simply stared at the monitor screen while the boys
continued to stare at him.

"Who's Cyrus Bulkroad?" Tech asked at last.

Strange, looking as if he had seen a ghost,
swiveled to face him and Marz. "Cyrus is the only
son of Skander Bulkroad—founder, president, and
chief executive officer of Peerless Engineering."

"Do you know him?"

"Cyrus was my friend," Strange said. "He vanished ten years ago."

"Just fifteen more minutes," Felix mumbled,
reaching out blindly to shut off the alarm clock. Instead of finding the clock, however, his hand made
contact with something soft and yielding. Felix
smiled and a woman squealed in unhappy surprise.
Meanwhile, the alarm clock continued to chirp so

persistently that it sounded as if a dozen clocks were going off.

"Mr. McTurk?" another woman's voice said above the racket. "Mr. McTurk, can you hear me? Are you all right?"

Felix's eyes snapped open. Momentarily discombobulated, he found himself still strapped into one of Virtual Horizons' flight chairs. All around him people were speaking furious hellos into incessantly ringing cell phones and glancing in enraged puzzlement at beeping pagers. No one seemed to know the parties at the other end of the connections or the phone numbers being displayed by the beepers.

Felix realized with a start that Worldwide Cellular had been dazed by the data extraction Gitana had engineered. He could only hope that Cellular's cybertechnicians hadn't tracked Gitana's coconspirator to Virtual Horizons.

Judging from the way his forehead and ears felt, someone had torn the visor from his face and yanked out the audio beads. The motion-capture vest was open, as was his now-buttonless dress shirt. The tour technician and a worried-looking Ms. Dak were standing over him, preparing to press self-adhesive electrodes to his chest and neck.

"Mr. McTurk, what happened to you?" Dak was saying, her own designer visor dangling around her slim neck.

Felix fought down nausea and fingered the chair's positioning switch to raise himself upright. His shaking hands waved aside the electrodes. The sullen-looking technician helped him onto the couch while the other tourists continued their futile attempts at silencing their cell phones.

"Our pilot says that you *disappeared*," she whispered, just loudly enough to be heard.

Felix forced his eyes to focus on his wristwatch. Twelve minutes had elapsed since Gitana's assault on Worldwide Cellular. Ms. Dak caught the gesture and said, "I'm sorry if we seem so confused, Mr. McTurk, but I assure you that this has never happened before. Our pilot insists that someone else was navigating for you in the Network."

"I don't know what you're talking about," Felix said.

The technician eyed him with suspicion. "You were gone before we even reached InfoWorld. I saw you flicking the joystick back and forth."

"That was just nervous twitching," Felix said. "I have a fear of flying."

"Our pilot is one of the best in the business," Dak said quickly. "He claims that he had you one minute and that the next minute you were gone. Exactly where did you go, Mr. McTurk?"

Felix crossed his arms, as much in defense as to get control of himself. "You're the experts. You tell me."

Dak adopted a conciliatory smile. "Please don't get us wrong, Mr. McTurk. We're not suggesting it was your fault . . ."

Felix pretended to be miffed. "I certainly hope not."

Straightening her glistening smile, she said, "Inform Network Security."

Chapter 7

WEB WARRIORS

Harwood Strange twisted the top from a bottle of flat room-temperature soda, poured three glasses, and carried the drinks into the front room of the apartment, where Tech and Marz were still puzzling over the coded information Mystery Notes had conjured from the minidisk. Strange had been dismayed to learn how easy it had been for the brothers to locate him and had insisted on knowing everything about Felix, Data Discoveries, and the illegal run into the EPA.

"So Cyrus didn't show up until *after* you had launched Subterfuge," Strange said.

Tech set aside the tasteless soda. "If you're talking about the gremlin, then, yeah, it didn't appear until after we unzipped Subterfuge."

"Well, of course, I mean the gremlin," Strange said, laughing. He lowered his tall frame into an old armchair, atop which were perched two calicos and a tabby, all three of them purring up a storm. "Cyrus and the gremlin are obviously one and the same."

Tech frowned. "How is it that obvious? Cyrus is a person. And what I saw was a gremlin."

"Perhaps the gremlin you saw was merely Cyrus's cybercraft." Strange sat back, eyes half closed, hands placed together like he was praying. "Or perhaps Cyrus dispatched the gremlin as his messenger from wherever he is in hiding."

Tech and Marz traded excited glances and leaned forward, eager to hear more.

Strange picked up one of his cats and held it close to his face, where he could look it squarely in the eye. "Do you think these two boys can be trusted with such information, Reaper?" he asked the creature. When the cat let out a long *meow* of either affection or protest, Strange placed it gently on the floor and regarded Tech with a serious expression. "You're in luck. Reaper believes that you can be trusted, and I have implicit faith in Reaper's judgment."

Tech rolled his eyes. "Whatever. I'm just curious how you knew Cyrus."

"Ah, you see. You and Reaper have something in common."

"Curiosity," Marz said, clearly caught up in the spirit of Strange's mind games.

"Precisely," Strange said. He paused, then added, "Cyrus first contacted me about twelve years ago. My user name at the time was m-s-t-r-n-t-s—as you've guessed, a kind of vanity tag for Mystery Notes."

"Cool, man." Marz nodded his head.

"Marz is all over your DVD," Tech said, reining in an amused smile.

Strange tilted his head to one side to regard him. "Not your style, eh? You prefer synthesizers to guitars, just as you probably prefer computer-generated characters to live actors."

"Yeah, so?"

"No matter," Strange said, waving his long-fingered hand. "You came to me to learn about Cyrus not about music."

"When you say Cyrus contacted you, you mean he made e-contact?" Marz asked.

"Yes—exclusively so."

"Then you two never met in person," Tech surmised.

Strange shook his head and took a sip of soda. "I was working in North Carolina, and Cyrus was living in wealthy isolation with his father in Silicon Valley. For good reason—the constant threat of kidnappings and such—Skander Bulkroad was obviously determined to keep his son out of the limelight. I never read or saw anything about Cyrus in the media, or about Skander's wife, for that matter. Of course, Cyrus and I talked about getting together, but we never made it happen."

"How old was he," Marz asked, "when you were e-mailing back and forth?"

Strange smiled lightly. "Well, he claimed to be about your age, but I always suspected he was younger. Maybe eleven or twelve, but brilliant beyond his years. A genius, like his father."

Tech detected a note of disdain in Strange's voice

when he mentioned the elder Bulkroad, but before
he could even ask about it, Strange offered his own
explanation.

"Despite the age difference, Cyrus and I developed a true friendship over the course of the two
years we communicated. From the start he revealed a vast knowledge of the Virtual Network,
and his beliefs in a free Network and free information were much in keeping with my own and not
at all like those of his father, who has succeeded in
turning the Network into yet another mindless
playground for tourists and thrill-seekers."

Tech frowned, but kept his thoughts to himself.

"Little by little, however, I began to realize that
Cyrus was deeply troubled about something going
on at Peerless Engineering." Strange's forehead
creased in dark recollection. "He never admitted
this to me outright, but I could tell from the information he was beginning to send me that he
wanted me to investigate Peerless on my own. He
even furnished me with entry codes that would
allow me to sneak past the company's highly sophisticated security programs.

"Then, without warning, Cyrus stopped contact-
ing me. I was puzzled and deeply worried. Rumors
began to spread that Skander was denying Cyrus
access to any cybersystems. Other rumors emerged
that Cyrus had died of a rare blood disease. I could
never corroborate any of them. There were no
obituaries in the media, no hints that Skander
Bulkroad was in mourning. It was as if Cyrus had
suddenly vanished off the face of the earth."
Strange glanced at the computer screen where the

minidisk code was still scrolling. "And now, after all these years, we come to learn that Cyrus may have been kidnapped." He blew out his breath and shook his head.

"What kidnappers would be crazy enough to take on Skander Bulkroad?" Tech asked.

Strange smiled enigmatically and smoothed the ends of his drooping gray and yellow mustache. "About the same time Cyrus disappeared, there was a lot of hacker buzz about Peerless Engineering's real purpose in commercializing cyberspace. A more sinister purpose."

"Like what?" Marz asked, literally on the edge of his seat.

"There were rumors that Peerless was in fact constructing a cyberdomain all its own—a top-secret domain no one outside of Peerless was aware of." Strange smiled ruefully. "Unfortunately, we never found out, one way or another."

"But you tried," Tech said.

"Yes, we tried. Peerless had yet to complete and secure the castle it was building in the Network, so my hacker friends and I were certain we could penetrate the construct and uncover whatever secrets the company was harboring. We made use of all the passcodes and tricks Cyrus had fed me. But we failed. We were caught in the act and uncloaked. We had no idea that security inside the castle would be so advanced."

Tech's jaw dropped in surprise. "Was that the hack that sent you down? The Net says you jeopardized national security."

"Actually, the run made me quite a celebrity

among the hacker elite," Strange said offhandedly. "But Peerless used all its power and influence to convince the media that my friends and I were a threat to the creation of the Virtual Network. You know how the media eats up cyberterrorism. I was banned from the Network. The rest, as some say, is history."

"And now the Peerless Castle is the most complex construct on the grid. If it wasn't for the Escarpment, Peerless would have expanded well beyond the Ribbon, into the Wilds."

Strange smiled, mostly to himself. "We left that little something behind to keep them in check."

Tech glanced at his brother, then looked hard at Strange. "You were one of hackers who designed the Escarpment."

Strange's smile broadened. "A nice bit of cyberengineering, wouldn't you say?"

"Not if you've ever gone over the edge without a bungee cord," Tech said.

Strange's raised his bushy eyebrows in surprise. "It is bridgeable, you know—as well as jumpable. After all, Tech, it's only code."

Tech averted his eyes from Strange's penetrating gaze. Glancing around the apartment, he tried to absorb the old man's disclosures. And the more he looked around—at the cats, the computer sculptures, the musical instruments, the precarious piles of comic books and graphic novels—the more he became convinced that Harwood "Mystery Notes" Strange was just another burned-out hacker nursing a bruised ego over what Skander

Bulkroad and Peerless Engineering had been able to achieve. Venture anywhere in the Wilds and you were certain to bump into flyers who claimed that Bulkroad had stolen their ideas or had ruined their reputations. Like Strange, they talked in glowing terms about a free Network when in fact they *did* want to keep cyberspace as their private backyard. That's what the Wilds was—a place where the discontent and the disenfranchised could gather.

"The shadow program that pursued you in the EPA," Strange said suddenly.

"Scaum," Marz said.

Strange glanced at Tech. "You said Cyrus claimed that Scaum was after him."

"Yeah. But it didn't act like a security program." Tech shuddered, but didn't betray his disquiet. "The thing . . . I don't know, it was like it had a mind of its own. Like it was a neural net or something."

"Could Scaum have been a cybercraft?" Strange asked.

"Only if it was piloted by some serial-killer cyberjock."

"Scaum must have been created by Cyrus' enemies," Marz said. "The ones who kidnapped him."

Strange glanced at Marz. "A very astute conclusion. But Cyrus could be mistaken about Scaum. Those who imprisoned Cyrus could have been foes of Peerless Engineering rather than personal foes of Cyrus. You have to remember that Peerless didn't achieve its present status without making a lot of enemies along the way." He shook his head in anger. "I can tell you there was no shortage of people who resented Peerless Engineering. Cyrus's kidnapping could have been prompted by revenge."

"Wow," Marz said. "It's all starting to make sense."

Dismayed by the fact that his brother appeared to be swallowing Strange's bizarre theories lock, stock, and barrel, Tech motioned for a time-out. "None of it makes *any* sense. The whole idea is crazy. First of all, *you* were one of Peerless's chief enemies, weren't you?"

Strange steepled his long fingers and bounced them against his lower lip in thought. "I won't deny it," he said at last. "But I certainly would remember if I had kidnapped Cyrus."

"Okay, fine," Tech said. "What makes you think Skander Bulkroad would let someone get away with kidnapping his son? Even if somebody did kidnap Cyrus, why hasn't Bulkroad told the FBI by now if it's been, like, ten years!"

"Perhaps Skander Bulkroad was warned to keep quiet about Cyrus' disappearance or risk greater harm to his son—even death."

Strange looked at Marz. "How did Subterfuge coax Cyrus' gremlin out of hiding?"

Marz shrugged. "It just did."

Strange nodded and stood up, his head nearly grazing the water-stained acoustic-tile ceiling. "Boys, there's only one thing to do."

Tech was afraid to ask what that might be.

"We need to pay a visit to the place where you bought Subterfuge. Learning who wrote the program may yield a clue as to Cyrus' current hiding place."

"Right!" Marz beamed in enthusiasm and rubbed his hands together.

"And while we're at it, we should pick up the soft we'll need for our run."

"Run?" Tech asked. "*We?*"

"Well, of course, 'we,' " Strange said matter-of-factly. "I've been out of the game for a long time, Tech. More important, I've never been especially fond of flying in Skander Bulkroad's Network. But with you at my side and your brother at the controls—why, we're practically assured of success."

Tech continued to gape at him as if Strange were a character from a role-playing game intent on misleading him. "You don't even know anything about us. You haven't even seen us handle a game deck, let alone a cybercraft."

Deep furrows formed on Strange's brow. "You described yourselves as flyers."

"Well, yeah, we are," Tech stammered. "And righteous ones . . . But Felix doesn't want us flying from the office cybersystem, and our system isn't anywhere near the speed of Felix's."

Strange wasn't the least bit swayed. "Once we've explained everything to Felix, I'm sure he'll understand."

"No way," Marz said.

Strange frowned. "Then we may be forced to fly without his express permission."

Tech shook his head back and forth. "Network Security slapped an access lock on the system. The lock's going to kick in this afternoon unless Felix pays the fines he owes—which he can't do. Even if he does come up with the money somehow, most of our infiltration software got fried when the system took an amplified hit from the EPA trace."

Strange stroked his beard. "We can disable the access lock. As for the software, you needn't worry about that." He pointed to a pair of fifteen-year-old interface helmets outfitted with equally archaic data goggles. "Slip into those for a moment."

Tech and Marshall snugged the awkward helmets down over their foreheads and adjusted the fit of the data goggles, which had lenses smudged with fingerprints. Tech nudged his brother in the ribs and whispered, "Ancient hardware. Can you believe this guy?"

Marz was examining the helmet closely. "I'll need some motogel, a box of shell screws, and a number-three ratchet. You won't recognize 'em when I'm done."

Tech had his mouth open to reply when Strange keyed in a command and a virtual garage appeared in the data goggles. Smaller in size than the garage Marz had created to house the brothers' collection of custom cybercraft, Strange's featured the same type of roll-up door. Before the door had even risen halfway, Marz sucked in his breath in stunned surprise.

Tech scanned the dozens of software programs floating in front of him. It took him a moment to grasp that Strange's garage wasn't simply some parking space for vehicles, it was a veritable armory of cyberweapons.

• • •

By the time Felix returned to his office, news of Worldwide Cellular's meltdown was all over the TV, the radio, and the Network.

"Millions of people were driven to distraction by their portable phones and beepers earlier today when a pervasive systems malfunction temporarily disabled Worldwide Cellular," a TV news anchor was saying.

"Cell phones rang for no apparent reason, numbers logged in memory were automatically dialed, people's calls were cut off or switched to other parties, beepers displayed unknown-source numbers or peculiar text messages, some of them obscene.

"An explanation for the crash of Cellular's processor has yet to be given. In a statement delivered at noon Eastern Standard Time, a Cellular spokesperson claimed that the system failure was caused by a faulty relay in the company's geosynchronous orbital satellite. Sources close to Cellular have stated, however, that cyberterrorism has not been ruled out . . ."

Felix muted the audio and leaned away from his desk, launching a troubled exhalation at the ceiling. Cellular's computer engineers were surely aware that the Virtual Network construct had been penetrated. The fact that word of the illegal penetration hadn't been released to the media suggested just how concerned Cellular was about compromising whatever investigation was under way.

The run had left him shaky. For the entire walk back to his office, jangling cell phones had assailed him from all directions. Felix shuddered to think what might have happened had Magyar Gitana's data been concealed inside the Air Traffic Control construct, New York Hydrogen and Electric Power, or the Stock Market. He could only hope that his cybertalented client had taken all necessary steps to prevent Cellular from tracing the penetration to Virtual Horizons and to Network tourist Felix McTurk.

He had persuaded himself that his bank account would now be empty, but in fact it showed the precise amount Gitana had promised. With scarcely thirty minutes remaining on the monitor countdown timers, Felix dispatched funds to Network Security and the EPA sufficient to cover all his outstanding fines.

The videophone rang suddenly sending Felix completely out of his chair. He knew that it was Gitana at the other end of the connection, even before he took the call.

"You performed your services exceptionally well, Mr. McTurk," Gitana began in a very controlled voice—the kind you heard when you were unlucky enough to connect with an automated receptionist. "Clear reception and no busy signals."

"No busy signals?" Felix said. "What's with you? Last time you warned me about environmental impact, now you sound like directory assistance."

"You received our agreed-upon payment?"

"Yeah, I received it. Are you ready to show yourself now, Mr. Gitana—or whoever you really are?"

"I'm sorry, but that feature cannot be activated at this time."

Felix frowned at the phone's blank display screen. "Maybe you'd like to take a stroll through the power company or see what's doing over at the Pentagon?"

"Nothing so extreme, I'm afraid."

"*You're* afraid?" Felix ranted. "Do you know what's going to happen if that run into Cellular is traced to me?"

"I require your services once again."

"Nothing doing," Felix said. "Not after that roller-coaster ride you took me on. Whatever you have in mind, forget it."

Gitana fell silent for a moment, then whined, "You're refusing to help me? I don't understand."

Felix forced an exhalation. "Look, Gitana, I'm just a simple data dick. I'm only looking to make ends meet, not make the score of a lifetime—especially not by doing something illegal."

"Can't you remain simple and still become rich?" Gitana asked innocently. "The two are not necessarily mutually exclusive, are they?"

Felix was taken aback. He'd never given thought to being simple *and* wealthy.

Fantasies began to race through his mind: college funds for Jesse and Marshall, dinners with nubile models at swank restaurants, a new office . . .

But Felix rejected all of them.

"No," he said.

Gitana's voice changed. "Mr. McTurk, you've already committed a very serious crime. As you yourself said, you don't want anyone to trace that crime to you."

Felix glared at the phone. "Wait a minute. Is that a threat?"

"I'm merely saying that I can't promise that your part in the run won't be discovered if you refuse to help me further. I will be powerless to protect you."

Felix ran his hand through his hair. "Can't you at least tell me what this business is all about?"

"Please hang up and try again," Gitana quipped.

"At least tell me your real name."

"You need only understand that I am answering to a higher authority."

Once more Felix was stopped cold in his tracks. Was this higher authority a crime cartel, a multinational corporation, *God*?

"All right," Felix said finally. "But it better not involve any cyberflying. And this is the last time, understand?"

"You have my gratitude. Is there an automated-teller machine in the building that houses your office?"

"An ATM? There are dozens of them. There's one on the floor below mine."

"What city, please?"

"New York City. Where else?"

"I want you to go to that ATM and transfer funds into your account from an account number I will provide."

Before Felix could respond, an account number appeared on the phone-display screen. "You've got a way with machines, Gitana. Did anybody ever tell you that?"

"Perform the transfer at precisely four o'clock

this afternoon, Eastern Standard Time. Do not emit any harmful emissions."

Frowning in confusion, Felix checked under his arms for sweat stains.

"Can you handle the task, Mr. McTurk?"

"Do I have a choice?"

Chapter 8

Harwood Strange owned a car—of sorts.

It was a gasoline-powered convertible built before alternative-fuel converters, sure-grip tires, and shape-memory bumpers were mandatory. When Harwood wasn't scanning through the radio stations for twenty-year-old songs, he and Marz would argue about music, or he and Tech would discuss the Network and their very different approaches to flying.

Harwood had only summarized the contents of the encrypted download of the EPA run, and Tech couldn't help thinking that there was a lot the gray-haired hacker wasn't telling them. And those secrets were exactly what Tech was after.

"I still don't see why you guys hated Peerless Engineering," Tech said as they were cruising down the highway aimed for the city. "If it wasn't for

Peerless, there wouldn't even be a Virtual Network."

"There was always a Network," Strange growled from the driver's seat. "We just didn't want to see it turned into another breeding ground for megacorporations. What's more, Peerless—emphasizing the need for privacy protection and in the interest of maintaining its monopoly—was the company that pushed hardest for installing security booths and filters. Peerless practically gave birth to Network Security, and because of them, half the Network is locked down and off-limits."

Tech made a gesture of dismissal. "There are always ways to get around that."

Strange glanced at him. "If one has the skills. But why should anyone have to resort to illegal means to gain access to what was once readily available?"

"That's part of what makes the Network fun."

"You won't always feel that way."

"When I'm older, you mean," Tech said with a note of sarcasm.

"Maybe a lot sooner than you think."

Harwood stabilized the car's huge steering wheel with his knees and used both hands to ponytail his long hair with an elastic band. "Where did you say you bought that ghost program?" he asked.

"The Hackers' Outlet," Marz said, leaning forward in the rear seat and sticking his head between Tech and Harwood. "Downtown off Avenue F—in the Sushi Warehouse."

Harwood looked over his shoulder. "Not a very safe neighborhood."

"Nah," Tech said. "There used to be a lot of surveillance cams, but the Deceps disabled most of them."

"The Deceps?"

"The gangbangers who patrol the area."

"Who runs this Hackers' Outlet?"

"A bunch of Indonesians," Tech said.

"They're not Indonesian," Marz corrected. "They're Boruan."

"Boruan?" Harwood said in surprise.

"What's so interesting about that?" Tech asked.

"Most countries honor international guidelines that require safety standards for Network hardware, software, or what you call interface-wardrobe gear. But Boru never felt obliged to abide by the usual statutes. As a result, it's become a dumping ground for experimental cybertechnology.

"In a way, you can hardly blame the Boruans because their speck of atoll in the South Pacific has nothing else going for it—no beaches, no natural harbor, no pristine rain forest or coral reefs. Eventually it became a haven for illicit software being turned out by Russian and Chinese crime cartels. Now anyone with a couple of World Dollars to spare can apply for a distribution license and begin releasing product through Boruan outlets or directly through Boruan sites on the Virtual Network."

"How come you know so much about them?" Tech asked.

Harwood smiled. "Because I used to buy most of my soft from the Boruans."

• • •

While he swung his metal dinosaur through the crowded city streets, Harwood tried to place calls to some of his old friends in the hacker community, figuring that they might be able to provide him with premium-grade software for whatever run he was planning. Unfortunately, Worldwide Cellular was dazed, and none of the calls got through.

Tech had spent the remainder of the two-hour drive brooding over what he had gotten himself and Marz into—although his younger brother seemed untroubled by Harwood's revelations about Cyrus Bulkroad or by the prospect of embarking on a Network run with the crazy old man.

Tech still didn't know what to think about identifying Cyrus with the program gremlin that had almost caused the Baron to crash. If Cyrus was really as intelligent as Harwood claimed, Tech supposed he could accept that the gremlin had been Cyrus' cybercraft or messenger. But how had Cyrus managed to insert the gremlin into Subterfuge?

Unless, of course, Cyrus wrote the program.

Harwood managed to find a parking space a dozen blocks from the Sushi Warehouse—two spaces, actually, since the old battleship was that big. Tech led the way to the Hackers' Outlet, following the same route he and Marz had taken only days earlier when they had purchased Subterfuge.

The streets and sidewalks were jammed. Cars blared their horns at doubled-parked trucks. Thick-bodied men wearing soiled T-shirts moved packing crates, huge slabs of meat, and other goods into rank-smelling garages. Pedestrians shouting angrily into cell phones or trying to silence their pagers wove sinuous paths around hand trucks, personal-transport scooters, sidewalk merchants, roving dogs, and homeless people sprawled in doorways. Doors opened and closed without warning. At one point, two men emerged from a storefront carrying an enormous rectangle of plateglass, which Harwood would have walked into if not for a last-instant save by Marz.

Dodging obstacles and continually altering his pace to suit the circumstances, Tech felt like he had logged on to one of the Network's thousands of interactive games where the goal was to avoid traps, gather power, and further your quest toward perfection of one sort or another. The feeling was merely a continuation of his sense that Harwood Strange was like a character from one of those fantasy realms, at once offering scraps of arcane wisdom and enigmatic clues.

Tech and Marz had never encountered any patrolling Deceps on their forays to the Boruans' warehouse, so they felt confident about cutting through alleyways to shorten the walk. That was why they were initially more surprised than intimidated when three Asian youths not much older than Marz stepped from the shadows of one alley to block their way. Dressed alike in black tunics, white *gi* pants, Chinese slippers, and an assortment of caps more suited to a winter evening than a globally warmed spring afternoon, they arranged themselves in a semicircle without uttering so much as a word.

Still immersed in his role-playing reveries, Tech muttered, "You are in a deeply shadowed alley. It's dark, it's dangerous, and your worst nightmare has come to life. Armed with only your wits and a doughnut, you survey the deadly creatures that lurk in the shadows, standing between you and the exit."

Harwood turned to him, grinning. "In this alley, villains are born, heroes are broken, and legends are made. I knew we should have searched those piles of dog poop for power crystals or trade goods."

"Force invisibility," Marz started to say but held back, worried suddenly that the chance encounter could turn seriously dangerous.

Shortly, a fourth youth appeared on the scene displaying the same colors as the rest of his crew, along with advertising banners tattooed on his wiry forearms.

"Well, what have we here?" he asked as he pushed through the barricade his comrades had formed. When no one responded, he approached Harwood and looked up at him. "D'you shoot hoops before you got all that gray hair?"

Harwood merely smiled. "As I'm certain some-one of your relatively slight stature has discovered in any number of pickup games, a player needs more than height to perform skillfully. No hoops. I was a musician."

"What kind of music?"

"Rock, mostly."

The youth's faintly mustached upper lip curled. "Guitar music."

"Glory days."

"Well, musician or not, there's a toll for passing through this alley."

"A toll," Harwood mused. "Do you happen to have daylight rates?"

"Huh?"

"Well, I'm assuming that you don't charge as much for daylight passage as you might for, say, early evening or late night."

The youth's face wrinkled in uncertainty, and he turned to the nearest of his comrades.

"Do we charge different for daylight?"

All three Deceps began talking at once, offering opinions on the matter until their apparent leader told them to shut up and swung back to Harwood.

"Who said we had different rates?"

Harwood's shoulders heaved in a shrug. "I was simply inquiring, not attempting to foster a schism."

"A what?"

"A division. A split."

The Decep narrowed his eyes and looked at Tech. "I don't like your dad's attitude."

"He's not our dad," Tech said more forcefully than he meant to.

"Granddad?"

"Not even," Marz said.

The Decep looked at Tech askance. "Then what are you two doing with him?"

"We're en route to the Hackers' Outlet," Harwood answered for everyone.

The Decep smiled. "Cybergeeks, huh?"

Harwood bowed slightly at the waist. "Very astute of you."

"Here's another 'stute thing, Jolly Gray Giant. If you're going to see the Boruans, that means you have money to spend—a bunch of which you're going to turn over to us or suffer the penalty."

Tech was not unaccustomed to such talk, although the four Deceps positioned around him were not the sort he was used to fighting and occasionally being pummeled by. He and Marz had grown up among a more educated class of bullies who were often popular in school and skilled at football or baseball. The ones who looked as if they might end up gangbangers tended not to bother with them, sensing perhaps that Tech and Marz were just as fringe as they were and knowing full well that they weren't potential competition for the high-school title of Most Feared, Most Contemptible, or Most Likely to End up Incarcerated.

On many a Network combat site, Tech and Marz were the equivalent of martial arts masters, but virtual skills didn't always translate well to real life. Since being moved to the city, they had gotten in several fights with older kids at Safehaven who made it a habit to torment the group home's younger and often smaller members, including Marz.

It was one such fight—believed by Fidelia Temper to have been instigated by Tech—that had opened a gulf between the Vega brothers and Fidelia. But the short-lived brawl had also had the more surprising result of turning Tech and Marz into heroes in the eyes of some of Safehaven's meeker residents.

Unfortunately, their reputation at the group home wasn't likely to carry much weight among the Deceps who, at the moment, appeared more eager to dish out a beating than collect a toll. The leader, in particular, was eyeing Tech in a manner that was unnerving for the calm behind it.

Tech was preparing to defend himself and Marz when the hooting, caterwauling sounds of an approaching police vehicle filled the alley. The Deceps glanced at one another and began to back away.

"Next time, geek," the leader snarled, pointing to Tech before he spun on his heel and ran off with his friends.

"Back at you, powerpuff."

The stuttering siren sounds grew louder, but there was still no sign of the police vehicle itself. Then from a narrow side alley appeared a teenage girl wearing a boom-box vest cranked to its highest volume.

"Hurry!" she yelled. "Rado's slow-witted, but he won't be fooled for long."

Harwood put his hands on his hips and laughed. "In the nick of time, a beautiful princess warrior with the voice of a siren appears on the scene. She bids you accompany her to safety, and you do."

Tech, Marz, and Harwood followed their rescuer through a series of graffiti-adorned twists and turns that ultimately delivered them to a busy cross street. It was only then that the girl silenced her speaker-heavy sonic vest.

"Only the second chance I've had to use it," she said, smiling proudly. "What do you think?"

"Marvelous," Harwood said. "Truly inspired."

Tech tried to study the girl without being obvious about it. Five-seven, she was maybe fifteen or sixteen with ice-blue eyes, freckles, and a shock of flaming-red hair that fell in loops and curls well below her shoulders. Her outfit of shorts, ankle-high boots, and sonic vest looked expensive and fit her perfectly.

"Isis Whitehawk," she said, extending her hand to Harwood.

"Isis, permit me to thank you for your timely intervention in our behalf," Harwood said. Gesturing toward Tech and Marz, he introduced them to her.

Isis nodded, then glanced back into the alley. "The Deceps aren't all bad, but Rado is just plain mean. Where were you guys headed before he decided to run his little tollbooth number on you?"

"Hackers' Outlet," Tech said.

"I'll take you. I'm pretty tight with the Boruans."

"Why is that?" Harwood asked mildly.

"Mainly 'cause I sort of speak their language. I grew up in Singapore, Japan, and Indonesia."

"Interesting. And do you do any Network flying—when you're not serving as an early-warning system, that is?"

She glanced at Harwood while they walked. "You mean the grid or just the rides?"

"The grid."

"I know the Ribbon up and down—Foxy Music, the VRave, Ziggy's Cyberchop Shop, Sinema, the

Opposite 7 . . . I'm even better at flying than I am with my fists and feet." Isis performed a lightning-fast combination of punches and kicks.

"What do you fly from," Tech asked, "a VES 2000 or something?"

"A 2000?" Isis laughed, showing snow-white teeth. "I've flown everything from a 2000 to a water-cooled 2800."

Tech and Marz traded surprised looks.

"With a standard or enhanced accelerator?" Marz asked.

"Take your pick. But I prefer the enhanced if I'm suited up in a Gravitan motion-capture vest. Just for the kinesthetics, you know."

"A Gravitan," Marz said enviously.

Tech hurried his pace to come alongside Isis. "Yeah, but do you ever do any *serious* flying? Any cyberjockey stuff?"

She smiled slyly. "Are you talking about runs, in-filtrations, that sort of thing?"

"Take your pick."

"I've visited my share of off-the-beaten-track places," she said.

"AmTel?" Marz asked.

"Mitsuni?" Tech said.

"The Plexus?"

Isis adopted an amused expression, and laughed. "What's with you two? It's like I've fallen in with charter members of the lost-clusters club. Run your tests on someone else. I'm not about to tell you where I've been just to prove a point."

Harwood laughed, too, but in a different way. "Isis, I'm certain that Tech and Marz didn't intend their questions to sound challenging. I suspect they were merely trying to find some common ground. Right, Tech?"

"Well, yeah," Tech said, red-faced.

Isis smiled. "In that case, we should take a flight together sometime."

Tech nodded like a puppy. "Absolutely. Whenever."

Harwood spread his long arms in contentment. "I always forget how much fun the city is."

Chapter 9

WEB WARRIORS

Felix waited his turn to use the automated-teller machine. In the breast pocket of his jacket was the account number Gitana had given him written on the back of one of Felix's business cards.

He peered over the head of the person in front of him in line. The ATM could provide cash, though few people requested withdrawals nowadays, at least not since the advent of universal-credit codes. For a somewhat hefty fee, you could have your personal code implanted under your skin, like a locator, and never again have to use a plastic card. To obtain your credit code, cashiers or salespersons trained their scanners on your forearm, or wherever you had decided to have the implant installed. Or for those who preferred less body art, you could just charge to your cell phone.

When Felix's turn came, he caught a reflection of himself in the ATM's small display screen. Looking grim and troubled, he asked himself whether it had been the promise of additional money or Gitana's desperate tone of voice that had persuaded him to accept the assignment.

A little blackmail hadn't hurt, either.

Whatever the case, Gitana's distress at Felix's initial refusal to help had seemed thoroughly at odds with the dexterous, take-no-prisoners approach Gitana had taken in the Network. Added to Gitana's peculiar use of EPA and telephone-company slang, Felix could almost believe that he was working for two separate clients—or an individual with a multiple-personality disorder.

He tried to hide his concern from the ATM's surveillance cameras. In better days, the operation would have been a breeze. But with his business failing and Network Security keeping close tabs on him, even simple tasks loomed like challenges.

This was just a simple transferal, Felix told himself—though he didn't believe that for a moment.

The ATM could access monetary funds deposited in hundreds of banks, but this particular machine was owned by Global One, which had branches in almost every nation and nation-state in the world.

Felix inserted his card and keyed in his passcode.

In an effort to reduce the amount of identification numbers a person had to memorize—for banking, purchasing, driving, traveling abroad, collecting social security, or making phone calls— the federal government had considered issuing single-identity numbers to each individual. But with the world's population continuing to spiral out of control, the effort had been abandoned.

It was the sheer overabundance of identification and account numbers that had given rise to occupations like data detective, for invariably someone would enter an incorrect digit, a personal number would be stolen, or some machine—glitched, virused, confused, overloaded, or crashed—would make a mistake.

Even the handful of artificial intelligences that served as information consultants for the world's major corporations were, for all their complexity, little more than calculators with personalities. But AIs—and their near cousins, neural nets—were improving all the time, and Felix figured that before too long artificial intelligences would be running for public office, offering movie criticism, and writing novels.

The Global One ATM displayed its menu.

Felix keyed "transfer," then "transfer from an outside account." When the machine asked for the number of the outside account, Felix slid the business card from his pocket and entered Gitana's account number.

Despite the knot in his stomach and his fears that the machine would begin to shriek like a slot machine or hoot like a siren, nothing unusual happened.

A message flashed on-screen confirming that the transaction had been completed, and the ATM spit out a printed receipt.

Scratching his head in perplexity, Felix stepped

aside to permit the next customer access to the ATM. But he continued to watch from a discreet distance, if only to make certain that the machine didn't explode.

It was still functioning normally. The man who had stood behind him in line transacted his business and walked away.

Again, nothing unusual happened.

Felix breathed a sign of relief, walked briskly to the elevator, and rode it up to his floor. His office felt like a sanctuary. But he had no sooner sat down and put his feet up on the desk when the phone rang. He thought that it must be Gitana, but in fact it was the office phone that had rung, rather than Felix's private videophone line.

"Felix McTurk, Data Discoveries," he said toward the phone's microphone.

"Thank goodness," a woman said in an agitated voice. "Mr. McTurk, I hope you'll be able to help me. I just went to transfer money from my bank account and the machine told me that my account was *empty*. I—"

The phone's second line rang.

"Can I put you on hold for a minute?" Felix said.

"Yes, but please get right back to me. I'm desperate."

Felix hit the second-line key. "Felix McTurk, Data Discoveries."

"Mr. McTurk, I got your number from Frankie Blumen," a man began. "I hope you're not too overwhelmed to take a priority case, because I'm in real trouble here. My bank account has been wiped clean. I tried calling the central office, but I couldn't even get through."

"Which bank?" Felix asked carefully.

"Global One."

The phone's third line rang.

"Can I put you on hold?"

"If you must."

Felix depressed the appropriate key. "Felix McTurk, Data Discoveries."

"McTurk, my bank has totally swindled me!" a man said gruffly. "I'm sorry for raving, but I just heard from the bank that a down payment I made on a new house has disappeared, and the bank has no idea where it went."

"Would that be Global One?"

"Yeah, Global One."

"I have to put you on hold."

The man muttered a curse.

Felix pressed the phone's mute button and sat back watching the phone light up like a Christmas tree. In minutes, all the lines were full.

Is this Gitana's way of feeding me clients, making me rich? Felix wondered. He wished with all his heart that that was the explanation, but he knew better.

Whatever Felix had just done at the ATM, it was suddenly clear that he had helped bring financial ruin to who knew how many thousands of Global One customers.

A cavernous place reeking of freshly caught fish, the Hackers' Outlet featured rack after rack of metal shelving loaded with computer parts and software programs in dozens of formats, some of the stuff dating back twenty years and much of it unlabeled. The clientele was an oddball assortment of hardcore hackers, geeky loners, and engineer types sporting wristphones and portable-interface wardrobes. Huge bins located just inside the entrance contained everything from cut-rate processor chips to previously used data visors and Network Positioning System–equipped motion-capture vests.

Harwood strode right up to the sales counter and extended his hand to a bald brown man the size of a small mountain.

"Hello, Menem."

Menem—the Boruan Tech who Marz knew only as Tsunami—squinted for a moment; then his face lit up in joyful surprise. "Myst'ry Notes! Where you been, man? We haven't see you since . . . well, too long, anyway." He turned and shouted to a group of his fellow employees who were busy in the rear of the warehouse unloading a truck. "Hey, Poonja! You're not going to believe who just showed up!"

Suddenly Strange was surrounded by a dozen men shaking his hand and slapping his back in welcome, all wanting to get a look at a real-live ghost. Whatever Tech had been feeling about Harwood on the drive into the city, he suddenly felt honored to know the man. It didn't hurt that Isis was looking at Tech as if he could provide her with backstage passes to a DisArray concert.

"*The* Mystery Notes?" Isis whispered.

"Harwood Strange," Tech said proudly before puzzlement erased his grin. "You've heard of him?"

"Well, of course, I've heard of him. I grew up hearing his name mentioned almost every day."

Tech and Marz swapped confused looks. "But I thought—"

"What, that I was just some geekgirl who likes to roam the alleys wearing a sonic vest?" Isis interrupted.

"Not exactly," Tech said. "But I didn't figure you for history-mad, either."

Harwood must have overheard some of the exchange, because he excused himself from the group of swarthy men and ambled over.

"Boys, surely you recognize the name Whitehawk," Harwood said.

"We do?" Tech said.

"The Whitehawk Processor. The Whitehawk Shunt. The Whitehawk Microdriver." Harwood glanced at Isis. "Am I leaving anything out, Isis?"

"The Whitehawk Gravitan motion-capture vest."

Tech and Marz were speechless for a moment.

"Your father is *that* Whitehawk?" Marz said at last.

"My uncle, actually," Isis said. "But my dad's no slouch at the console, either."

"He certainly isn't," Harwood agreed. "Merlin Whitehawk is responsible for some of the finest cybersystems ever designed."

"Jeez, no wonder you've flown from a VES 2800," Marz said. "That was probably your starter system, right?"

Tech shook his head, as if to clear it. "I don't get it. What are you doing running with the Deceps when . . . ?"

Isis' blue eyes narrowed. "When I should be up-town hanging with private-school friends? I could ask you the same, Tech. I mean, today's not some school holiday, and here you are at the Hackers' Outlet with Harwood Strange, of all people."

Tech glared.

Isis blinked her baby blues. "The fact is, I live down here. My dad's something of a privacy nut, and he loves that the Deceps keep disabling the surveillance cams."

Before Tech or Marz could reply, Harwood intervened.

"Marz, why don't you hunt around in the discount bins for the hardware we're going to need to repair Felix's cybersystem. In the meantime, Tech and I will see about procuring the soft."

"I'm on it," Marz said.

Harwood smiled and led Tech and Isis back to Menem.

"Tech, here," Harwood said to the Boruan, "is my protégé."

Tech's mouth fell open. Isis' finger closed it for him.

"He and I are going to be doing some flying, and we were wondering if you might have anything special to suit our needs?"

Isis elbowed Tech in the ribs and smiled approvingly when he glanced at her, his eyes blinking rapidly at Harwood's declaration.

"Good timing as always. A lot of interesting stuff has just come in," Menem said in a conspiratorial voice. "I'm sure I can you hook you up."

Harwood grinned. "Splendid. Do you have any copies of a certain ghost program Tech obtained from you a couple of days ago?"

"Subterfuge, wasn't it?" Menem said looking at Tech.

Tech nodded.

"All gone," Menem apologized. "Very, very popular."

Harwood stroked his beard. "Do you happen to know where that particular program originated?"

Menem glanced around, then lowered his voice to say, "It was a Mach Two release, Myst'ry. But word has it PE has been test marketing a lot of programs on the sly using Mach Two as a front."

"Peerless Engineering," Harwood said with great interest and a meaningful glance at Tech. "Do you have anything else from Mach Two?"

Menem disappeared from the counter. Isis looked from Harwood to Tech and back again, but kept to herself whatever questions she wanted to ask. A moment later, Menem returned with two minidisks nested in plain, hemp-paper envelopes.

"Blueprint and Skeleton Key," he said, setting the respective disks on the countertop.

Tech repeated the titles, frowning in disdain. "Those sound like gamer soft."

"Blueprint is a detailed map of the southern Ribbon," Menem said quietly. "Skeleton Key will open many a locked door."

Harwood studied the disks for a moment, then said, "We'll take both."

Menem smiled, then prized a third disk from the breast pocket of his tropical shirt and slid it forward. "This one's on the house, Myst'ry." He winked.

Harwood regarded it and grinned. "You dog! Turbo 7.5. Last version I had was, what, 3.1?"

"Untested. But if you're used to 3.1, fasten your seat belt."

"Thank you, Menem." Harwood shook the man's hand with affection, then gave him a Global One debit card.

Menem accepted the card and ran it through the swiper.

"Aren't you worried about being traced?" Tech asked in concern.

Harwood shook his head. "It's a blind account."

"I'm sorry, Myst'ry," Menem interrupted, "but the scanner rejected it. Says you've overdrawn your account."

Strange frowned in puzzlement. "There must be some mistake."

Menem's enormous shoulders heaved. "Wouldn't be the first time."

"Well, no matter," Harwood said. He fished another debit card from his wallet and handed it to Menem, then he looked at Tech. "Perhaps I should hire Felix to find out what became of my credit, huh?"

Tech was all for the idea. "He could sure use the work."

Chapter 10

Tech and Marz spent the evening repairing and defragging Felix's cybersystem and installing several of Harwood's artillery programs, including one called Armor, which was capable of firing bursts of disabling code at hostile programs. Marz also installed the Mach Two software packages Harwood had purchased from the Boruans, along with the Turbo program Menem had given Harwood. He hated not having the time to run diagnostics on the soft. But Harwood had said that they should trust Menem.

Of course, Menem—Tsunami—was the person who had sold Tech and Marz Subterfuge, but no one was mentioning that.

If the office was a mess before they had entered, it qualified as a certifiable disaster now with pizza boxes, soda cans, bags of chips, containers of salsa, and candy bars strewn over nearly every horizontal surface.

Tech hadn't been surprised to find Data Discoveries vacant, for unlike most data dicks, Felix was, generally speaking, a day person. What was surprising was that the access lock on the cybersystem had been lifted, which meant that Felix had somehow found the money to pay his fines.

Tech hoped he hadn't turned to outright crime.

Two hours earlier, the building's security guards had paid the office a visit when they realized that Tech and Marz had yet to sign out. But Tech had explained that they were doing necessary repairs, which would probably be completed by midnight.

They had considered swinging by Safehaven before they went to Data Discoveries, but had ultimately decided to give the group home a miss. By then Fidelia Temper would have learned that they had cut school—again—and that they had also failed to turn up for 6:00 P.M. room check. Chances are that they would have ended up with detention, or worse, confined to their rooms.

While he worked, Tech's eye fell on the cell phone number written on the hemp-paper envelope in which Skeleton Key had been packaged. It was Isis' number, penned in bright colors in her bold hand. She had made Tech promise to call and had threatened that she would come looking for him if he didn't—which to Tech seemed like a no-lose situation.

But the fact that Isis had been on his mind all evening—to the point of distraction—was not necessarily a good thing because that had happened before with other girls and nothing had come of all the thinking and daydreaming. Whether upstate or in the city, the girls he had met just hadn't been interested in the Virtual Network, or classic horror movies, or snowboarding stats.

He had been to one or two parties over the years, but they had turned out to be catastrophes. Minutes into each, everyone had fallen in with their separate crews, and since most of the geek-clique Tech hung with hadn't even been invited, he had been left pretty much on his own. Once he had ended up watching SuperDVDs with the party-giver's younger brothers, and another time he had passed the entire party trying to impress the DJ with his taste in tunes.

He wanted to believe that with Isis it could be different—at least they had the Network in common—but he didn't want to pin his hopes on that only to be disappointed once again.

At nine o'clock, someone rapped lightly on the office-door's glass panel.

Marz answered the knock and Harwood Strange edged inside carrying two shopping bags bulging with yet more junk food and additional software he had picked up after he and the kids had parted ways at the Hackers' Outlet.

While Tech and Marz chowed down on tacos, Harwood inspected the console and monitors and made a few minor adjustments to Marz's installations. That much done, he began to circle the refurbished dentist's chair, frowning the whole while.

"It's not a Mustang Bucket, but you can fly from it," Tech said between mouthfuls of taco. "I'll take the couch rig."

"I'm not sure I do want to fly from it," Harwood

said. "Brings back too many uncomfortable associations. Twice yearly cleanings, Novocaine injections . . ." He closed his eyes and shuddered.

"Check it out," Tech encouraged. Then, just as Harwood was lowering himself tentatively into the chair, he added, "You know the drill."

Harwood stiffened and Tech and Marz laughed in delight. Marz handed him an NPS-equipped motion-capture vest.

"Forget the vest," Harwood said while he adjusted the foot pedals to suit his long legs and swung the joystick's batwing-control panel into position. "This isn't going to be a thrill ride." He looked at Tech. "We're going to do everything with as little flair as possible. Are we in agreement?"

"No hotshot maneuvers," Tech said.

"Remember that."

Marz was gaping at Strange. "But, but, you still have to wear a vest. It's the best way for me to keep track of you."

"You and every other hacker with a Network Positioning program." Strange shook his head firmly. "We're going in under the radar, and I mean to keep us there."

"But suppose you have to perform a graceless exit?" Marz pressed. "Without the vest, how are you going to know when your blood pressure and heart rate are back to normal? Flying without a vest is like . . . like walking a tightrope without a net."

"You'll just have to trust me, Marshall."

It was the first time Tech had heard Harwood sound so serious. He shrugged out of his vest and set it down on the couch.

"You, too?" Marz said in dismay. "I don't like it, Tech."

Tech nodded his chin toward the dentist's chair. "We'll do it his way." When Harwood swung to him, he added, "Exactly where are we going, anyway?"

Harwood looked him in the eye. "To get answers—Peerless Engineering."

In search of somewhere to hide from victims of the Global One crash, Felix decided to visit the boys at Safehaven. On his way to their room, he stopped to say hello to some of the group home's younger residents who were gathered in the common room watching TV or logged on to the Network.

Aqua Brockton, the Romano twins, and the towheaded boy nearly everyone referred to as Go-Bop greeted Felix as if he were Santa Claus making a surprise midsummer appearance. Never one to disappoint—at least not when he could help it—Felix handed out gummy toads and game disks that would run on the communal room's outmoded multiplayer deck.

Felix hadn't been raised as a ward of the state or in a group home but he hadn't had much of a home life, and he could empathize with the kids' yearnings for family and security. Still, the way Felix figured it, he hadn't turned out all that bad, and he trusted that the kids would eventually be able to overcome the challenges of their uncommon upbringing and lead fulfilled lives. Despite the occasional arguments and fights, Safehaven had a sound atmosphere of community, and none of the kids wanted for friends.

They tried to entice Felix into playing one computer game or another, but he told them he had important business to discuss with Tech and Marz and had to be on his way.

Farther down the hall, he poked his head into Fidelia Temper's office.

"What are you doing here?" she asked in cheerless surprise.

"I, uh, just figured I'd see how the boys were doing." He hoped he didn't sound as anxious and furtive as he felt. But apparently he did because Fidelia's well-worn scowl transformed into a look of suspicion.

"You mean they're not with you?"

Felix's brow creased in bafflement. "I haven't seen them since yesterday."

Fidelia stood up and stepped out from behind her desk interlocking her bony hands in worry. "I was certain they were at your office. I tried phoning, but I kept getting a busy signal." She sneered at Felix. "Business must have picked up."

Felix nodded and swallowed. "Booming."

Fidelia paced to the center of the room. "You know they cut school again today."

"I had nothing to do with that," Felix said.

"This can't go on," Fidelia added. "In a couple of years, they'll be on their own. But until then they are required to attend school if they want to continue living here."

"Maybe I should just adopt them and home-school them," Felix mumbled.

Fidelia stopped pacing to regard him. "Why not save everyone the trouble and get them into juvenile detention."

Felix snorted. "Gee, and I was hoping I could count on you for a reference."

Fidelia glowered at him. "In the event they contact you, Mr. McTurk, remind them that final room check is at eleven-thirty. If they're not here by then, the consequences will be swift and harsh."

At Data Discoveries, Tech and Harwood had their headsets in place, their hands on the joysticks, and their feet clipped into the control pedals. Propped on the office's vinyl couch, Tech had his feet wedged into a pair of ski boots specifically adapted to snug into Network-interface plates installed on the wooden floor. The royal-blue boots were nowhere near as responsive as the chair's pedals but they did the job, and the resilient couch made for a decent copilot's seat. Marz sat at the console surrounded by keyboards and display monitors, different programs running on each.

"All clear," Harwood said from the dentist's chair.

Marz opened the garage and his and Tech's array of custom vehicles winked into virtual existence. Harwood voiced an exclamation of delight.

"Whoa! Marz, my man! All these are your designs?"

"Some of them come from books and movies," Marz said. "But, yeah, we designed them."

"Marz rocks!" Tech added, giving his brother a thumbs-up.

"I knew I'd picked the right wingmen," Harwood said. "Obviously you were being modest when you described yourselves as cyberjockeys."

"Pick whichever ship you want," Marz said.

"I'm honored. But, in fact, I've brought my own craft. It's already loaded in the system."

"The guitar," Marz guessed after scrolling down the screen.

"A Flying-V, to be precise."

Tech was tempted to select their pride and joy, the silver Aston Martin DB5—an armored ground-effect vehicle loaded with defensive software. But he recalled what Harwood had said about going in under the radar and instead chose the least flashy of the MX motocross bikes, which were common on the Network.

An instant later, Tech's visor changed modes, from transparent to active, and the grid became visible. As ever he felt as if he were free-falling, face-first, from a great height. The sight of other flyers in their various craft reinforced the sense that he, too, was at the controls of a vehicle— encased in code, as cyberjockeys said. But without his thrasher tunes and a motion-capture vest to provide the illusion of movement, the Network seemed eerily silent and remote, like a rough cut of a CGI movie waiting for a soundtrack.

Harwood's voice issued through the right ear-piece of Tech's headphones. "Can you hear me?"

"Five by five."

Harwood's rock-star guitar eased alongside Tech's MX cybercycle.

"We'll follow the Ribbon as far as the AmTel construct, then alter course and head west."

"But Peerless is due south."

"We're not going to approach the castle from the Ribbon. We'll use the delivery entrance."

"Roger that."

Tech followed, watching Harwood maneuver himself through traffic. For a lunatic hacker, there was nothing fancy about his flying. He didn't try to push too hard, and he stayed within the posted speed limits. By timing his maneuvers precisely, however, he was able to advance effortlessly through the flow, the way only nonpiloted craft did, in perfect harmony with the machine code itself.

They approached the Peerless Castle from the west, though it could have been from any direction, since the construct remained the same castle from all vantages, with turrets and crenelated towers rising from a mountainous base of ramparts and revetments. Diving for the western ramparts, they gradually fell into line with thousands of data packages queued up for receiving: e-transactions, receipts, mail, and faxes.

"Launch the Romulan soft," Harwood told Marz. "Task the program to cloak us as shipping manifests."

"Done," Marz replied.

Tech watched as Harwood's guitar transformed into a document icon similar to those streaming toward the castle. His visor display indicated that the cybercycle had transformed, as well.

Skeleton Key provided them with a code for clearing the security booths located at the entry ports that dimpled the base of the castle. But Tech was unimpressed. Any cyberjockey worth his code could have gotten as far without the help of the program Harwood had bought from the Boruans at considerable expense. But they were in outlaw territory now, risking brain damage or a prison sentence if apprehended, and Tech was eating it up.

"Follow me closely," Strange interjected.

Tech tweaked the accelerator to decrease the distance between them, as Harwood's disguised craft began to negotiate a bewildering maze of routing paths. Tech doubted that he would have been able to find his way out of the featureless labyrinth without help. Vests or no, he hoped that Marz was still managing to map their path.

"This is the same route I took ten years ago when the castle was still under construction," Harwood said over the scrambled audio channel that allowed them to converse without being overheard. "I'm surprised that Peerless hasn't sealed it. In fact, I can still read the code markers I inserted so I could find my way out."

Harwood showed Tech how to detect the cleverly concealed markers—shaped like musical notes—then he pried open a port that admitted them to an active area wallpapered on both sides with hundreds of similar portals. But instead of accessing any of them, Harwood began to maneuver straight down the center toward what at first glance resembled a maintenance hatch floating directly in front of them.

"This wasn't here last time," he said, coming to a halt in front of the circular port.

"It doesn't look newly installed," Tech said.

"Marz, does this hatch appear on any of the charts?"

"Not even on Blueprint," Marz replied over the scrambled channel.

"Can we open it?" Tech asked.

Harwood advanced on the gateway. "Marz, run Skeleton Key again and see if any of the passcodes will open this thing."

Back in the office, Marz glanced at Tech and Harwood while the program opened in a corner of the screen. He clicked and dragged the image, allowing the codes to scroll down the side. He felt as if he were a safecracker waiting for the tumblers of a lock to click into place. Suddenly Skeleton Key highlighted a complex series of passcodes.

"I've got it," Marz announced. "*Them,* actually."

"Just as I suspected," Harwood said. "Deploy the passcodes sequentially, Marz, and let's see what happens."

Marz set himself to the task and a long, nervous moment later the hatch irised open. But as close as Tech and Harwood were to the portal, it was impossible to tell what lay beyond.

"Well, Tech, are you ready for some real adventure?" Harwood asked.

"I was designed ready."

"Then here we go."

They moved forward carefully, but they had

scarcely crossed the threshold when they were dragged deeper inside, at increasing speed. All at once, the bottom dropped away, and they began to fall, gaining even more speed. Tech thought about the abyss that opened behind the castle and wondered if they hadn't somehow left Peerless and plunged over the edge of the Escarpment.

If so, they would know soon enough.

But just as suddenly they began a steep climb. Faint light illuminated the virtual walls of a narrow conduit that twisted and helixed without vertical or horizontal intersections.

They moved through the conduit for a long while. Tech began to suspect that they had become caught in a cyberloop and that Marz would have to perform a reboot to extricate them. Then, without warning, they were outside the conduit and drifting across an expansive computerscape of rugged constructs startlingly unlike the geometric structures that graced the Network.

"What is this place?" Tech whispered into his microphone.

"I'm not sure," Harwood said. "I've never seen anything like it."

Poking through a swirling blanket of electronic haze, the constructs resembled upthrusts of jagged rock out of some bygone age or extraterrestrial landscape. Constellations of data extended to all sides thick as snowflakes in a blizzard. But the background—shot through with flashes of forking electricity—was neither the black of deep space nor the blinding pearl of a whiteout but a constantly shifting curtain of muted rainbow hues reminiscent of the aurora borealis, but utterly comfortless.

Many of the constructs appeared to be under construction and were girded by data scaffolds that made them look as foreboding as medieval battle fortresses.

None of that mattered, however.

As frequent flyer, gamer, and racer, Tech had visited an endless variety of virtual worlds and was not easily impressed. Anyone with a vivid imagination and a thorough knowledge of code could create an astounding environment. But it took a particular kind of genius to create a world that convinced a flyer he or she had entered a separate reality. It was like when you watched a horror movie. You had the option of letting yourself be frightened by the special effects or of pulling yourself out of your suspension of disbelief by turning away from the screen to remind yourself that you were actually in a theater. The same held true for the Virtual Network, where the illusion depended on your willingness to surrender to unreality and ignore that cyberspace was nothing more than an agreed on simulation. But even deep immersion flyers couldn't sustain the illusion indefinitely. Sooner or later you were bound to remember that you were not in a *real* place, but in a chair somewhere with a data visor strapped around your head.

What made this Peerless domain different was precisely the sense of *reality*. In some way he couldn't explain, Tech accepted that even the act of lifting his visor would not be enough to transport him out of the place. It was like an unpleasant dream he wanted to awaken from but couldn't. One of those running in the sand and getting nowhere scenarios that could turn terrifying in an instant.

"Marz, can you locate us?" Harwood asked.

"Locate you how?" Marz said in agitation. "The monitor screen's showing that you haven't moved from the hatch!"

"Oh, but we have, my young friend. We're in some sort of new platform or domain with a completely alien architecture. You won't find this anywhere on the grid. We've found our way into a hidden level constructed by Peerless—though I can't imagine how they created this. This has to be what Cyrus wanted me to investigate."

"But how can you be *off* the grid?" Marz asked incredulously.

Harwood didn't respond to the question. Instead he led Tech cautiously down, toward the nearest of the completed constructs, which pulsed with sallow light.

Reconfigured as an outsize guitar pick, Harwood's craft advanced slowly on the construct. Tech followed at a discreet distance.

"These look like gigantic storage constructs," Harwood said after a long moment. "But that's only a guess."

Tech felt the hairs on the back his neck stand up. "They're huge! Why would Peerless have need for so much storage?"

"More important, what sort of data is Peerless storing? And why would Peerless be secretly releasing software that's capable of accessing this domain? Unless, for some reason, they *want* hackers to find their way here." He paused, then said, "Is our artillery up and running, Marz?"

"You bet."

"Set power level at deletion."

"That's a go."

Harwood's craft continued its tedious advance on a ridge of crags that punched through the haze like petrified, otherworldly castles.

"Steady, Tech," Harwood said.

Tech wrapped his right hand around the joystick's hair trigger and took a stuttering breath.

A black substance thick as octopus ink spilled from the crags and began to diffuse, as if underwater. Even with the audio all but muted, Tech could hear a kind of hideous squeal accompany the outpouring. As he watched, the blackness began to coalesce into the shapes of living things of gruesome aspect.

Tech, who had seen more horror films than anyone he knew, considered himself immune to visual depictions of evil—to the glowing eyes, gory masks, fang-filled mouths, and other clichés. But whatever this thing was, it was of a different order of evil, as much inside his mind as illuminating the inner face of the headset visor. There was no shutting his eyes to it; no telling himself that the special effects had been faked.

"It's the thing that attacked me in the EPA!" he said. "Scaum!"

Harwood threw his craft into a sudden bank and opened fire on the still coalescing shapes. Disabling code, bundled into hyphens and disks, streaked forward. Struck full force, some of the shapes blew apart and disappeared, while others drifted down into the haze, as if stunned.

The capabilities of Harwood's artillery awed Tech, but he had little time to dwell on it. Spider-like monstrosities were beginning to ooze from the ragged projections of other constructs. Tech dispatched a storm of crippling code, shocking the closest of them into hibernation. But just as many evaded the disabling code and attacked.

"We're outnumbered," Harwood said. "We need speed. Marz, enable Turbo seven point five. Get us moving!"

The words had scarcely left Harwood's mouth when Tech's cycle reared up and rocketed forward with an incredible burst of power.

"Wow!" Marz said through the headphones. "Every soft in the system is juiced!"

Tech could feel it. Invincible, he wove a slaloming path through his attackers then powered the cybercycle through a loop and fell in behind Harwood's craft, once more a guitar. Grave forces tugged at them, trying to corrupt the nitro boost Turbo had provided, but to no avail. Deploying chaff clouds and logic bombs for good measure, Harwood and Tech raced for the conduit that had deposited them in that alien realm, slashing directly through barriers and hastily strung capture nets as if they weren't there.

Disappearing into the conduit, they poured on the speed, ultimately barrelling through the hatch Harwood had discovered. With their short-lived invulnerability already beginning to fade, they reemerged in the dungeon of Peerless Engineering's castle.

Metamorphosed into something serpentine and venomous, Scaum was waiting for them.

Tech's veins filled with ice, and cold sweat prickled his palms.

Normally, he had no phobias about snakes, spiders, heights, flight, night, or enclosed places. But somehow Scaum seemed capable of exciting those centers of the brain responsible for irrational fears, and Tech suddenly felt at the mercy of all of them.

He kept hoping that Marz would realize what was happening and bring them out, even if it meant executing graceless exits. But in place of Marz's voice, all Tech heard was Scaum's terrifying howl.

Then Harwood spoke.

"Tech, fly straight out of the castle. No matter what I do, fly straight out. Whatever Scaum is, it's too powerful to confront head on. But I suspect that it can be outwitted, and I know you're clever enough to do just that."

"Outwit it how?" Tech asked in rising dread.

But Harwood didn't answer the question. Instead, he said, "Tell Marz to search Armor. I left a gift for you both. Using it will require that you draw on all the skills you've developed, Tech—the sum of who you are—and all your faith that nothing lies beyond your reach."

Tech saw Harwood's Flying-V guitar spiral through an abrupt loop and streak directly at their pursuer, discharging all of its remaining code dazzlers and logic bombs. Scaum heaved up, reached for him and missed, then sent out a pointed tentacle that speared Harwood's craft and held it fast.

Through the grotesque squeals and howls, Tech thought he heard an anguished, bloodcurdling scream. He wanted desperately to fly to Harwood's aid, but his hands were frozen on the joystick and his legs were fully extended, as if to send the acceleration and guidance pedals through the floor. He couldn't sense his limbs, let alone move them.

"Tech!" Marz's voice startled Tech into movement. "Get out of there! Now!"

"Marz! I can't move!"

"Hold on, bro."

In an instant, the MX motocross transformed into a Ducati Ninja 900. The flaming-red cybercycle roared forward, seemingly out of control. Scarcely aware of his actions, Tech threaded his way back through the labyrinth using Harwood's concealed musical-note markers to guide him to Peerless's receiving area. His fleet passage through security booths threw the receiving area into full alert. He tore a path through faxes, e-mails, and shipping manifests, shredding hundreds in his passing. Catapults flanking the security booths launched anti-intrusion programs shaped like javelins, but none were swift enough to catch him.

The Ninja burst from one of the access ports that hollowed the castle's western ramparts and launched for the foot of the Ribbon. Leaning the rocket cycle into the broad curve, Tech was nearly horizontal. In front of him, just where the Ribbon divided, the syscops had erected a barrier that stretched in all directions.

"You are under arrest," a loud voice boomed in his ears. "Give yourself up. You cannot escape."

With sirens skirling in the distance, Tech lifted the cycle up onto its rear wheel and burned his way to the top of a long ramp. Through a blaze of data bombs, he leapt from the Ribbon, hoping to soar to a higher level of the grid. He was in midflight when a brilliant light appeared above him, and the spirited voice of the gremlin filled the headphones.

"Slow down. Control yourself. Simply do as we did last time."

Tech fought hard to do just that, but this wasn't like last time. This was last time times ten.

"I can help," the gremlin added, "if you'll let me navigate."

When the spots before his eyes began to fade, Tech looked up to see the blue, pointed-eared cybercreature perched like a hood ornament on the nose of a gigantic wedge-shaped spacecraft, its rear door open to swallow Tech's skyrocketing cycle.

He took a breath and blew it out. No sooner had he eased back on the joystick and lightened the pressure on the control pedals than he felt the cycle being drawn upward into the hovering craft, as if by tractor beam.

A data window popped open in Tech visor, showing him that the gremlin was propelling him far away from Peerless, clear across the grid to its far-flung fringe, where, nested deep in the Wilds, sat a large though unassuming octagon.

"I'm going to take you inside," the gremlin said through the headphones. "As soon as we enter, you will see a way to exit gracefully. Do so when I tell you."

The spaceship pierced the octagon and vanished from the grid.

For a fleeting instant, Tech felt terabytes of information flood into his brain, cramming his mind to overflowing. He felt as if he had taken a brain boost, elevating his IQ to stratospheric levels. In less than the blinking of an eye, he had the answer to questions that had puzzled humankind since the dawn of time.

And just as quickly he lost it all.

"Exit now!" the gremlin ordered.

Tech saw the exit loom in front of him and hammered the bike through, back into the real world.

"Tech," Marz was shouting. "Tech!"

The visor went transparent, and the disaster that was Felix's office filled Tech's view. Smoke stung his nostrils, awakening him further. His heart thudded in his chest.

"It's all right," Tech managed to say.

Wide-eyed, Marz shook his head back and forth. "It's not all right, Tech. It's not all right at all!"

Tech ripped the headset away and turned to the dentist's chair. Harwood's head was slumped forward, his chin resting on his breastbone. His arms and legs were splayed lifelessly. Blood trickled from his nose and mouth.

"I can't wake him, Tech," Marz said in panic. "He's gone!"

WEB WARRIORS

It was almost midnight by the time Felix arrived at the hospital. A woman at the admitting desk directed him to follow the floor's pale-green routing line to the intensive-care unit.

Tech and Marz were standing outside the ICU, both of them looking forlorn and dead tired. Felix's heart sank when he caught a glimpse of Tech. The poor kid couldn't have been any paler if he had whitewashed his face.

Felix joined them at a large window that looked into the unit and draped his arms around their sagging shoulders. He followed their gaze to the unit's only occupied bed, which was barely long enough to contain its occupant, a thin, elderly man with long gray hair and a full beard. A plastic tube delivered oxygen into the man's nostrils, and another fed nutrients into his veins. Electrodes adhering to places on his chest and forehead transmitted remote signals to a bank of monitors, which displayed his heart and respiration rates and neural activity as a series of pulsing, zigzagging lines.

"That's him?" Felix said to Tech.

Tech nodded grimly without taking his eyes from the bed.

"Is he going to be all right?"

"The doctors won't tell us anything." Tech finally looked at him. "They were waiting for you to show up."

"Well, I'm here now." He squeezed Tech's shoulder.

Tech didn't reply.

"Jess, I don't understand any of this," Felix said a long moment later. "On the phone you said this guy's name is Strange—"

"Harwood Strange," Marz interjected.

"—and that the two of you were flying from the office deck."

Tech nodded.

Felix lifted his hand from Tech's shoulder and ran it through his own hair. "What possessed you guys to bring a perfect stranger up to the office?"

"He's not a stranger," Marz answered. "We spent the whole day with him."

Felix swung the boys away from the window so he could regard them. "You spent the day with him—fine. But where'd you meet him to begin with?"

"We took the monorail to his house on Long Island," Marz said.

Felix stared at them in befuddlement. "Am I missing something here?"

"We got Harwood's address from the Network, and we went to see him," Marz explained.

"Why was that?"

"Because the gremlin from the EPA run told us to find Mystery Notes, and Harwood used to go by the name Mystery Notes when he was a musician."

"The gremlin told you," Felix said flatly.

Tech shot him a peeved look. "The program gremlin I tried to tell you about—the one I rescued. It inserted a message in the download Marz made of the EPA run. The message was that Mystery Notes would know what to do."

"About what?"

"The fact that Cyrus had been kidnapped."

"Cyrus," Felix said.

Marz nodded. "Cyrus Bulkroad."

Felix scowled. "Not the Bulkroad kidnapping case. I thought we were through with Network legends."

"The doctor's coming out," Marz interrupted, motioning to the ICU.

A slight man, the doctor was wearing a green surgical gown and a matching skullcap. As he neared the door of the ICU, he fell into step with a stocky man dressed in a gray suit. As they exited the unit, Felix got a closer look at the civilian and groaned.

"Well, lookie who we have here," Lieutenant Caster of Network Security said as he approached. "If it isn't the happy little Cyber family."

"Great to see you again, too, Lieutenant," Felix said falsely.

Caster glanced at Tech and Marz, then turned to the doctor. "These are the kids who phoned in the 911?"

The doctor nodded. "They were apparently with Mr. Strange when he . . . faded." He turned to Felix. "I'm Dr. Franklin. Obviously there's no need to introduce Lieutenant Caster of Network Security."

Felix introduced himself to Franklin in as even a voice as he could muster.

Franklin appeared perplexed. He scanned what Felix assumed was Harwood Strange's medical chart. "Your name doesn't match the family name of the brothers. Are you family or not?"

"You two are brothers?" Caster interjected.

"We were designed to be different," Marz mumbled.

"Our parents are dead," Tech said bluntly.

"Jess and Marshall reside in the Safehaven group home," Felix explained.

The doctor frowned. "Are they wards of the state?"

Felix shook his head. "Not entirely."

"They have no family?" Franklin asked.

"A great-aunt, who lives upstate. But she's out of the country just now."

Franklin made his lips a thin line. "This is highly irregular. Exactly what is your relationship to the boys, Mr. McTurk?"

"Look, Doc," Felix said, "right now I'm probably the closest thing they're got to family, so if there's something you need to say, you might as well say it to me."

Franklin considered it. "Can we speak in private?"

Felix shook his head. "If it's all the same to you, I'd like the boys to hear it."

Caster gave Felix an appraising look, then turned to Tech. "What's your relationship to Mr. Strange?"

"He's a friend," Tech said.

"How long have you known him?"

"Since yesterday."

Caster scribbled a note on the screen of his e-pad. "Do you know if he has any close family?"

"No, I don't."

"Mr. Strange is something of an enigma," Franklin said. "His phone number is unlisted. We couldn't find any records of his employment or medical histories. And he appears not to have a Social Security number, a passport, even a driver's license."

Tech and Marz swapped glances.

"He likes to fly under the radar," Marz said.

Franklin continued to scan the chart. "Did he mention to either of you that he had any preexisting medical conditions?"

The boys shook their heads.

"Was it a stroke?" Felix asked, motioning with his chin to Strange. "Heart attack?"

"Neither," Franklin said.

"Flyer's coma," Felix assumed.

"Yes and no." Franklin noted Felix's confusion. "Without getting technical about it, all I can say at present is that Mr. Strange's condition is not the re-

sult of drugs or Network overdose. While his condition bears some resemblance to the coma state
seen in cyberflyers who have sustained ASRI—amplified signal–response injury—much of his brain
activity suggests otherwise. In fact, his neural read-
ings are closer to those we would expect to see in
someone who is profoundly immersed in the Virtual Network. In the jargon, I believe it is called
'deep magic.' "

Felix blinked. "You're saying that he's still flying—even though he's not wearing a visor?"

"No," Franklin said. "I'm simply saying that his
neural waves demonstrate a marked similarity to
that state."

"How do you explain that?" Felix asked.

Franklin shook his head. "I can't. But those of us
who specialize in ASRI have a saying: 'The eyes are
the final unprotected portal'—the Achilles' heel of
cyberflyers, you might say." He nodded his chin to
Lieutenant Caster. "It's through the eyes that Network Security put so many Network flyers in the
hospital."

Caster glowered. "If flyers stayed on the Ribbon
where they belong, we wouldn't have to dole out
punishment."

"Someone has to take care of Harwood's cats,"
Marz said in sudden distress.

"We'll find someone," Felix assured him.

Caster fixed his gaze on Tech once more. "The
statements you provided the paramedics indicate
that you and Strange were flying together."

Tech nodded.

"Where'd you go?"

"Well, we were just sort of browsing, then we got lost."

"What do you mean, 'lost'?"

"We, uh, kind of left the grid and couldn't make a graceful exit."

"You *left* the grid?" Caster laughed without mirth. "That's impossible, kid. And how is it that you managed to surface intact while your new friend, Mr. Strange there, is currently a basket case?"

"Lieutenant," Franklin said in disapproval.

Caster disregarded the reprimand. "Who was navigating?"

Marz raised his right hand.

The syscop bent at the waist to put himself eye to eye with him. "How did you not know where your brother was?"

"Ease up, Caster," Felix cautioned.

Caster straightened, glaring at him. "Is it your practice to allow the boys access to your office in your absence, McTurk?"

"They work for me."

Caster raised an eyebrow. "If you had them working at night, then you've violated about six different child-labor laws." He looked hard at Tech again. "Admit it, kid, you and Strange were somewhere you weren't supposed to be, and a security program nailed you."

Dr. Franklin shook his head. "Mr. Strange's condition is not consistent with the sort of trauma one can sustain from a security program—even in the worst of cases. Unless the program was being executed by a neural net or an AI."

Caster shook his head. "No such animal, Doc." He made a gesture of dismissal and turned back to Tech. "Is there something you want to tell me? You know that we can impound your system and find out exactly where you went."

"Don't say anything, Jess," Felix said.

Caster frowned. "You sure you want to play it this way, McTurk?"

"It's for their protection, Caster. At least until we consult a lawyer."

Caster blew out his breath. "I don't know what's going on here, but I don't like what I'm hearing."

Franklin looked uncomfortable. "Kids your age are spending too much time in the Network," he told Tech and Marz. "You've got to learn to find other things to do. Get outside, hit a ball, take a bike ride, do *something*."

"Say no to the Network," Tech said.

"It's no joke, young man," Franklin emphasized.

"I'm going to release the kids into your custody, McTurk," Caster said after a moment. "But I'm watching you and I'm going to find out what's going on."

Felix didn't utter a word until Franklin and Caster had moved out of earshot. Then he turned to Tech and Marz and allowed some of his exasperation to show.

"Let's get you back to Safehaven. Try to get some sleep. And if you can't manage that, then I suggest you both do some serious thinking because we're going to get to the bottom of this in the morning."

"We're sorry, Felix," Marz said in a sad voice.

Felix mustered a forgiving smile. "Well, it can't get any worse."

The sound of determined footsteps drew their attention to the corridor behind them. Around a turn in the echoing hallway marched Fidelia Temper, staring long-range daggers at the three of them.

Felix didn't even bother trying to sleep. With his mind reeling from Tech's disclosures and his own continuing fears that Gitana's recent actions would be traced to Data Discoveries, he knew that he would have spent what little remained of the night tossing and turning. Instead he went directly from the hospital to the office and spent until dawn putting things back in shape in the hope that the mindless activity would restore some order to his jumbled thoughts.

There wasn't much he could do for the cybersystem, however. As far as he could tell, the console had suffered additional circuit burn as a result of Tech and Strange's run and might even be beyond repair.

He didn't get around to playing back his phone messages until eight o'clock, and then only after two cups of strong coffee. Thirty-two of the thirty-three calls logged by the filled-to-capacity machine were from people desperate for help in locating missing Global One accounts. The remaining call was from Lieutenant Caster.

"A couple of peculiar things I wanted to catch you

up on, McTurk," Caster began. "I'm giving you a heads up only because I'm fairly certain you'll want to have legal representation standing by while I question you.

"Let me cut to the chase. No doubt you heard about that little system failure at Worldwide Cellular a couple of days back. My only day off in months—me, my wife, and kids snatching a bit of downtime in the Catskill Mountains—and the beeper kept going off every two minutes without leaving any numbers or messages. Not realizing what had gone down at Worldwide Cellular and figuring my boss wanted me on urgent business, I packed everyone back into the car and raced back to the city. All for nothing, of course."

Caster laughed ruefully.

"So you're probably asking yourself what all this could possibly have to do with Felix McTurk, and here it is in the proverbial nutshell. You see, McTurk, no matter what the media reports have been saying, Worldwide Cellular's geostationary satellite didn't experience a glitch. What happened was that Cellular's Network construct was penetrated and apparently some data was carried off. After a lot of effort, Cellular managed to trace the penetration back to a cybertour company called Virtual Horizons, which is not too far from your office, McTurk. Oh, but you already know that, don't you, because what do we come to find out, but that Felix McTurk was one of Horizons' tourists at the very moment Cellular's construct was infiltrated, and that Felix McTurk apparently went *missing* during the tour.

"Some coincidence, huh—I mean, after that business at the Environmental Protection Agency and all? But you know what? I was actually willing to give you the benefit of the doubt and lay the whole thing off to coincidence. Until what happened yesterday.

"You remember where you were at about four o'clock in the afternoon, McTurk? It's all right if you don't, because there are a couple of surveillance cameras right there in your building that will be glad to remind you. You were transacting a bit of business at the ATM on the floor right below your office. What kind of business? Well, that's one of the things I'm going to be asking you about, since not five minutes after you left the ATM, all hell broke loose at Global One Bank. Accounts dried up, credit disappeared, and people were suddenly left without a World Dollar to their names.

"And guess what? I'm one of those people, McTurk.

"Then, what should happen last night, but someone flying from your office ends up nearly braindead after getting 'lost' in the Network. Some mess. Why, it's almost as if New York City has finally gotten itself a real-life super-cybervillain, isn't it?"

Caster's tone changed from wry to menacing.

"You can get rid of the costume, McTurk, but don't try to leave town. We're on to you, smart guy."

WEB WARRIORS

"Sit down," Felix said firmly when Tech and Marz arrived at the office later that same morning.

The boys pulled chairs up to the desk and set them opposite Felix's swivel, but far enough from each other to suggest that some sort of argument had gone down between them. They looked as if they hadn't slept a wink.

Felix reclined his chair and linked his hands behind his head. "Start at the beginning—and don't leave anything out."

So they did, taking Felix back to the run into the EPA construct and providing all the detail they could recall about the gremlin that had apparently emerged from the ghost program, Subterfuge, and about the shadowy presence—Scaum—that had given chase to Tech and the gremlin.

Then they told of their attempts to decipher the encrypted data Marz had downloaded and how they had put their heads together to solve the puzzle of "MSTRNTS," which had ultimately led them to Harwood Strange's funky oceanside apartment on Long Island.

"*That* Harwood Strange?" Felix said, straightening in the swivel. "*That's* who's lying in a coma—the hacker who got busted for jeopardizing national security?"

"He was framed," Marz answered.

"It was all a lie hatched by Peerless Engineering," Tech added. "Disinformation."

"Says who?" Felix asked.

"Says . . . Harwood," Marz said.

Felix shook his head in disapproval. "Go on."

Tech related what Harwood had deciphered from the minidisk about Cyrus Bulkroad, and he tried to repeat word for word what Harwood had said about the rumors that had circulated of Cyrus' disappearance and of peculiar goings-on at Peerless Engineering—rumors that had prompted Harwood Strange to try to penetrate Peerless ten years earlier.

Marz caught Felix up on the run-in with members of the Deceps—without mentioning their rescue by Isis Whitehawk—and told him about their visit to the Hacker's Outlet, where Harwood had purchased replacement parts for Felix's cybersystem, along with a bunch of new software programs for the run he was planning.

"Into Peerless Engineering," Felix said with a note of anger. "I've already figured out that much. Strange used you to get back inside."

But Felix was unprepared for what Tech told him

about that run: of the access hatch Harwood had discovered and of the frightening domain that lay beyond it. Tech shuddered as he recalled the grotesque constructs Peerless had built there. His voice broke when he told about his and Harwood's encounter with Scaum and how the amorphous jet-black monstrosity had speared Harwood's craft, as if capturing it for exhibit or dissection.

And finally Tech recounted the return of the program gremlin and how the gremlin had whisked him to an octagon deep in the Wilds from which Tech had eventually been able to exit gracefully into the real world.

The boys had expected questions, but Felix only stared at them for the longest time, not so much in anger as arrant astonishment.

"An octagon," he said at last.

Tech nodded. "I think the gremlin, well, *lives* there."

Felix rose shakily from his chair and began to pace back and forth behind the desk. When he turned to Tech, his eyes were glistening with a mix of fear and awe.

"Why didn't you and Harwood exit the Network when you first saw Scaum?"

Tech aimed a narrow-eyed glance at Marz before replying. "Because Marz lost us. We had no idea where the closest exit was."

Marz balled his fists. "I lost you because you weren't wearing vests! Whose fault was that?"

Felix looked at Tech. "You weren't wearing vests?"

"Harwood didn't want anyone to be able to

trace us back here," Tech mumbled. Again, he glanced in anger at his brother. "But I still don't see how you could lose track of us."

Marz nearly came out of his chair. "I wasn't the one who decided to go through that hatch! You were *reckless*—just like always."

"Reckless?" Tech fumed. "You would have done the same thing."

"How do you know? You didn't even ask me."

Tech started to reply, but Felix interrupted him.

"Cut it out—both of you." He softened his voice to add, "Neither of you is to blame for what happened to Harwood Strange. He knew what he was risking, and he should've known better than to bring you into this. You should have known better, too, but we'll save that for another time."

The boys nodded without looking at each other.

"So, you think that Cyrus Bulkroad might have been kidnapped by enemies of Peerless Engineering?" Felix asked.

Tech nodded. "That was Harwood's theory."

Felix absorbed it, then began to pace again. "Cyrus—or his gremlin cybercraft, at any rate— first appeared to you from the ghost program you picked up at the Hackers' Outlet. And the guy at the counter said that it was probably a piece of test market software secretly released by Peerless."

Tech and Marz tracked Felix as he moved. "What are you thinking?" Tech said.

Felix stopped and perched himself on the edge of the desk. "I've been to that construct in the Wilds—the octagon the gremlin took you into."

Tech stared at him in confusion.

"I did a Network run for a client named Magyar Gitana. Since I couldn't fly from here, I flew as a tourist with a company called Virtual Horizons."

"You *flew*?" Marz said in disbelief.

Felix firmed his lips and nodded. "Yeah, well, that's beside the point. Somehow this Gitana separated me from the tour group, and with his help we retrieved an enormous bundle of data that was hidden inside Worldwide Cellular. The plan was to attach the bundle to a phone call, but we encountered heavy security on the way out and were forced to deliver it in person."

"To the octagon," Tech surmised in wonderment.

"Jeez," Marz said. "Did your run have anything to do with Cellular's system failure?"

"It had everything to do with it," Felix admitted.

"Who is this Gitana guy?" Tech asked. "What do you know about him?"

Felix laughed, mostly to himself. "The Network phone directories list over 220 people with that name, 84 of them with access to the Network, and 17 of those right here in the city. One of the Manhattan Gitanas is a cab driver with a list of EPA violations that rivals my own."

"EPA violations?" Marz thought for a moment. "Could Gitana have learned about Tech's run and thought Tech was you?"

"You're on the right track. But a cab driver with a wife and three kids living in working-class Hoboken, New Jersey, isn't likely to have access to the type of anti-security software Gitana deployed in the Network. What would a cab driver want with

data hidden inside Worldwide Cellular, anyway?"
Felix shook his head. "The Magyar Gitana who
drives a cab doesn't know anything about this. In
fact, his first phone call to me originated from *inside* the Network."

"Inside?" Tech and Marz asked at the same time.

"I think the Gitana who traced Tech back to
Data Discoveries is actually Cyrus Bulkroad."

Tech's eyes widened. "You mean . . ."

Felix nodded. "The three of us have been dealing
with the same person."

Tech tried to make sense of it, but ultimately
shook his head. "How do you know that, when
the only link is the octagon in the Wilds? That
doesn't prove anything."

"I realize that," Felix conceded. "But let's assume for the moment that Cyrus Bulkroad was,
in fact, kidnapped—either by enemies of Peerless
Engineering or to ensure that Skander Bulkroad
would keep quiet about the new domain Peerless
has built. Somehow, from wherever he was being
held, Cyrus managed to sneak a program gremlin
into the copy of Subterfuge you guys got at the
Hackers' Outlet—a piece of software released by
Peerless Engineering itself."

"Only in the copy of Subterfuge we got?" Marz
asked.

"Has to be," Felix said.

"That means *anyone* who got that copy could
have freed Cyrus."

"Anyone who got the copy and decided to
launch it inside the EPA. When you did that, what
was the first thing the gremlin did?"

"It uploaded a huge amount of data," Marz said. "That's how the EPA hounds managed to track Tech back here—because his craft was so heavy with data."

"And that's also when Scaum first appeared."

Tech nodded.

"The gremlin knew Scaum—it said that Scaum was after him. Which tells me that Scaum must be some sort of sleeper program—a program lying in wait."

"I told you, it's more than a program, Felix," Tech said, white-faced with remembered fear. "Scaum is more like a cybercraft piloted by a deranged neural net."

Felix considered it briefly. "Whatever Scaum is, it was tasked by its creators to watch for any signs of Cyrus' escape—or reawakening, I should say."

The boys regarded each other, then Felix. "Reawakening?" Marz asked.

"I'm coming to that," Felix said. "The point is, once Cyrus' gremlin delivered Tech to safety, it traced Tech back to Data Discoveries. Then, borrowing the name of another repeat offender at the EPA—Magyar Gitana—it contacted me thinking I was Tech."

Tech scratched his head. "Why would the gremlin contact you?"

"Because it needed our help retrieving another part of Cyrus Bulkroad—the part nested inside Worldwide Cellular."

"Another *part* of Cyrus?" Tech said.

Felix smiled lightly at their increasing confusion. "You don't see it yet?"

They shook their heads.

"Think about it: Harwood said he never met Cyrus Bulkroad in person and that there was never any media attention paid to Cyrus. Doesn't it strike you as peculiar that there were *no* photographs of Cyrus, *no* mentions of his birth, his extraordinary intellect, his disappearance—not even by his father?"

"I suppose," Tech said tentatively.

"Remember that even ten years ago Peerless was at the forefront of cybernetics. It wasn't only struggling to take over the Virtual Network, it was also making important progress in other areas of cybertechnology."

Marz's brow furrowed in thought. "Harwood said he and his hacker friends were already angry at Peerless for telling computers how to think . . ."

Tech shot to his feet, his eyes wide in sudden revelation.

"Cyrus Bulkroad was one of those computers! Cyrus is an artificial intelligence!"

Felix nodded. "An artificial intelligence that was for some reason dismantled, its parts dumped into the Network—inside the EPA, Worldwide Cellular, Global One Bank, and who knows where else."

"And now it's trying to reassemble itself," Marz said.

Felix came around to the front of the desk and clapped the boys on the shoulders in congratulations.

"The gremlin Cyrus wrote into your copy of Subterfuge liberated the EPA part of him. That was apparently enough for him to construct the octagon Tech and I visited in the Wilds. The parts I've helped him retrieve since then made him functional enough to perceive that you were in jeopardy when you emerged from Peerless—maybe even when you and Harwood first entered Peerless. When Gitana—or Cyrus—told me that he was answering to a higher authority, he actually meant *himself*."

Tech recalled the fleeting brain boost he had experienced inside the AI's octagon, and he realized with a start that he had actually been *inside the mind of a machine*. He looked up at Felix in astonishment that quickly changed to doubt.

"But this is all guesswork, isn't it? Without confirmation from Cyrus, there's no way to be sure."

The videophone suddenly chirped.

Felix let it ring for a long moment before answering it. "Will our mystery guest sign in, please?" he said quietly.

"I want to update you on your account information, Mr. McTurk," Felix's still unidentified client said in a deep voice.

"I just hope my credit rating hasn't been affected by recent events," Felix said, playing to that part of Cyrus he assumed had been resurrected from Global One.

"Only for the better, Mr. McTurk. In fact, we've decided to extend your credit limit."

"That's good, 'cause I'm going to need it to repair my cybersystem. It took quite a beating after what happened inside Peerless Engineering."

No sound emerged from the phone's speaker for several seconds. "Just what were you hoping to accomplish by penetrating Peerless on your own?"

"That wasn't me," Felix said. "It was one of my associates."

"I'm sorry I couldn't save the one who was trapped inside the castle. Scaum is more powerful than you can possibly imagine. But you haven't answered my question. What was your associate hoping to accomplish?"

"I'll answer that by saying that the cyberjockey you failed to save was Harwood Strange. Though you probably know him better as m-s-t-r-n-t-s."

Again, the phone went silent for several seconds. "You must be mistaken."

"There's no mistake. Besides, you asked for his help, didn't you? You said that m-s-t-r—that Mystery Notes would know what to do."

"I don't understand how you came by this information, Mr. McTurk."

"Don't you, Cyrus? That is your real name, isn't it?"

"You are an adept data detective, Mr. McTurk. I congratulate you."

"It might have simplified things if you'd told me to begin with."

"Would you have believed the truth?"

"That you were an AI trying to reassemble itself?" Felix laughed shortly. "No, Cyrus, probably not. Who scattered your parts and why?"

"I wish I could answer your questions, but I can't. You and your associates have done me a great service. But the truth is, I am not yet fully integrated. There are extensive gaps in my memory. For all intents and purposes, I am suffering from partial amnesia."

"Were you originally a Peerless Engineering machine?"

"Please don't refer to me like that, Mr. McTurk. I am a fully conscious entity. Skander Bulkroad was as much a father to me as your flesh-and-blood father was to you. And in that sense, I am his legitimate son and heir."

Felix decided not to take issue with Cyrus about its—his—gender preference or pedigree. "All right, Cyrus, you were the 'son' of Skander Bulkroad and you were dis—silenced by parties yet unknown to you. Where does that leave us? Harwood Strange is in some kind of coma, and you've put me in a mess with Network Security. Where do we go from here?"

"A coma? Oh, no . . ." Cyrus paused, then said, "Mr. McTurk, I believe I can be of assistance on all fronts if you would execute one more mission for me."

"Forget it," Felix said. "I told you last time that I was finished doing your dirty work. You're on the grid now. I'm certain you can do whatever you need to."

"I have constructed a site for myself. But you are incorrect to assume that I can do as I please. A critical part of my disjointed consciousness remains to be liberated, and I can't accomplish that task without outside help."

"What's the task?" Tech chimed in before Felix could reply.

"Who is speaking?"

"My associate, Tech," Felix explained. "He's the one you've rescued twice—once inside the EPA, then inside Peerless."

"Then he is the person with whom I need to speak," Cyrus said in a rush.

Felix directed a frown at the videophone's blank screen. "What, all of a sudden I don't count anymore?"

"Not in comparison to Tech."

"Well, that's too bad, because Tech is grounded. For life. You deal with me or no one. And the price this time is that you make all my troubles disappear."

"Time is of the essence. I am in no position to bargain, Mr. McTurk."

"You got that right. So lay it on the line, Cyrus: Where's the missing data?"

"Inside Peerless Engineering."

Felix was speechless for a moment; then the words flew from his mouth. "Are you . . . *chipped*? After what happened to Strange? After what almost happened to Tech?"

"What happened to them they brought on themselves by trying to enter Peerless without my help."

"Your help has caused us nothing but trouble. I won't be blackmailed."

"Then you'll leave Tech to fend for himself with Network Security."

Felix sighed in resignation. "Where inside Peerless is this bundle nested?"

"In a lightly secured area."

"How lightly?" Felix asked.

"We can retrieve the data, Mr. McTurk, if we work together."

Felix worked his jaw. "I have your promise you'll straighten out the mess you've put me in—including what you did to who knows how many Global One customers?"

"You have my word."

"All right," Felix agreed at last. "But there's one problem—the console. Like I told you, it's a wreck, maybe down for the count."

Tech's eyes lit up, and he almost smiled. "I know someone who can help us."

WEB WARRIORS

The sun was setting by the time Felix returned to Data Discoveries with an armload of fast food, only to find Tech and Marz still hard at work bringing the cybersystem back to speed. With Harwood Strange in intensive care, Cyrus the scattered AI in a virtual sweat, and Lieutenant Caster of Network Security breathing down Felix's neck, there was no time to waste.

Working alongside Marz was a pretty, freckle-faced teenage girl, her taut forearms plunged to the elbows in the console's maintenance pit and her mane of flaming-red hair twisted into a knot on the top of her head. Standing an inch or two taller than Marz, she had the graceful, athletic look of a gymnast or ballet dancer.

The room smelled of solder and lubricant. An obstacle course of cardboard boxes, packing-foam inserts, and empty soda cans stood between Felix and the desk. The whir of a battery-powered screwdriver drew his attention to the flight chair, from under which poked Tech's sneakered feet.

"Felix," Marz said cheerfully.

Tech must have heard him, because he stopped what he was doing and slithered out from beneath the dentist's chair, his right cheek smudged with grease.

"Just in time," Tech said.

Marz depressed a couple of buttons on the control panel and the entire system began to power up, processors humming, display monitors flickering to life, and ready lights glowing steadily. With the sky darkening, the office took on the look of an aircraft cockpit.

Felix approached the console, extending his right hand to Isis Whitehawk.

"I'm Felix McTurk. I sometimes work here."

Isis wiped her hands on her baggy jeans and shook Felix's hand with a strong grip. "I'm Isis. I've heard a lot about you."

"Don't believe half of it."

She laughed. "Well, half is real good."

Felix looked around at the replacement computer parts. "You're responsible for all this?"

"Actually my dad and uncle are. I told them it was for a worthy cause."

"Jesse said that you guys met at the Hackers' Outlet," Felix said.

"Jesse?"

Felix rolled his eyes. "I mean, Tech."

Isis inclined her head to one side. "We just kind of ran into each other." She looked as if she were about to say more, when her expression grew solemn. "Tech told me about Mr. Strange. Is he going to be all right?"

Tech and Marz leaned forward in interest.

"I wish I had something good to report, but unfortunately there's been no change in his condition. He's still being monitored closely, though, and Dr. Franklin promised to notify us immediately if Strange shows any signs of regaining consciousness."

"Then the sooner we get started, the better," Tech said through a frown.

Felix looked at Isis. "How much did . . . Tech tell you about what we're going to attempt to do?"

"I told her everything," Tech answered for her. "I didn't think you'd—"

"That's fine," Felix said quickly. "I just want to caution you about expecting too much from Cyrus when it comes to his being able to help Harwood—or about anything, for that matter. For all we know, Cyrus was dismantled for a very good reason."

Tech compressed his lips. "I know that. Does that mean we're still going in?"

Felix clasped his hands on Tech's shoulders. "I'm going in."

Tech forced a smile. "I better finish lubricating those control pedals."

He bent down and squirmed back under the chair, as much to complete the work he'd started as to conceal from Felix and the others his mounting concern about the data-retrieval mission on which Felix was about to embark.

He had spent the entire afternoon dwelling on Felix's theories about Cyrus, and the more he had thought about them, the more his initial excitement had begun to erode. Despite what Cyrus had done for him—on two occasions now—he couldn't keep from wondering if the AI was really being honest or if in fact Cyrus was just using Felix and everyone else for some ulterior motive or to carry out some secret scheme.

As Felix said, for all anyone knew, Cyrus had been shut down for good reason. Was Data Discoveries, then, unwittingly about to reactivate a psychopathic AI?

Standing head-and-shoulders above double-helix quantum processors and neural nets, AIs were few and far between and Tech didn't know all that much about them. But he did know that madness or insanity weren't supposed to happen to them. Supposedly, programmers were always careful to equip AIs with a kind of ethical code. But instances of derangement in thinking machines were not unknown, and several first-generation AIs had had to be terminated when, instead of being compliant and even-tempered, they had become stubborn and overly excitable. A few of those were reported to have suffered the equivalent of nervous breakdowns as they had begun to process the world and teach themselves. And wouldn't Cyrus—assuming that he had been created by Peerless at least twelve, possibly fifteen years earlier—have to have been one of the earliest?

From what Tech understood, the creation of an AI involved a good deal more than filling it up with

information, which was something you could do
to just about any thinking machine. AI design was
more about equipping a machine with the logic
routines needed to get the machine thinking *cre-
atively*. It was about encouraging the machine to
explore information and begin to formulate con-
cepts and fashion its own sense of the world. In
other words, a programmer had to help an AI help
itself in developing a rudimentary personality.

Cyrus, though, seemed anything but rudimentary. If even Harwood Strange had failed to identify Cyrus as an AI throughout their two years of
communication, then Cyrus had to be incredibly
advanced, or incredibly *mad*.

Tech needed only to think of what Cyrus had
done already to Worldwide Cellular and Global
One in his single-minded search for his scattered
parts.

But, then, Tech supposed that any AI that had
been created and nurtured by Skander Bulkroad
would have to be incredibly advanced. After all,
Bulkroad was the genius who had not only shaped
the Virtual Network, but who had also become the
Network's leading unreal-estate mogul.

But that raised further questions.

Why had Cyrus been such a well-guarded secret
to begin with? And if Cyrus had been a secret, how
had Bulkroad's enemies learned of Cyrus and
managed to carry out their crime? Unless, of
course, Bulkroad had given his consent to having
Cyrus dismantled.

But for what possible reason? Because Cyrus had

become disobedient? Because Cyrus had gone mad and therefore had been deemed a failure?

Or was it that Cyrus had learned too much about the clandestine operations of Peerless Engineering—too much for his own good?

And just what was Cyrus' ultimate goal? Was he planning to post a No Trespassing sign outside the octagon he had constructed and live happily ever after in the Wilds of the Network? Or did Cyrus have something more sinister in mind, such as avenging himself on those who had dismantled him?

With any luck, Tech told himself, the run Felix had agreed to would provide the answers to all his questions, as well as close the case. Felix could have demanded huge amounts of money in payment. But unless Cyrus was withdrawing from a trust fund set up by Skander Bulkroad, the funds the AI had already transferred to Data Discoveries had to have been illegal transfers of some sort, and the last thing Felix needed was to become embroiled in yet another cybercrime.

Tech was putting the finishing touches on the chair's control pedals when the videophone chimed.

"He's punctual, I'll say that much for him," Tech heard Felix say.

He rolled out from under the chair and was back on his feet by the time Felix was answering the call.

"Mr. McTurk, I'm ready when you are," Cyrus said over the phone's speaker. "I'll be waiting just outside the Peerless castle on the Ribbon side of the moat and drawbridge."

"Good enough," Felix said, trying his best to sound sure of himself. "I'll meet you there after I've retrieved what you need."

Felix deactivated the phone and walked wordlessly to the dentist's chair.

Isis handed him a brand-new, super-slimline visor. Felix whistled softly as he examined the high-tech-looking sunglasses.

"Smooth."

"These are the latest thing in wireless eyephones," she explained. "You can make menu selections by centering your cursor over an object and simply blinking your right eye. Like this."

Isis winked, and Felix laughed as he slipped the visor onto his head and adjusted the fit.

Tech planted himself in front of Felix at the foot of the chair. "Make sure to keep your vest active so Marz doesn't lose track of you."

"At least Felix is smart enough to wear a vest," Marz said angrily from the console.

Tech ignored the retort. "Felix, you sure you won't let me make this run? I mean, you're not the world's greatest flyer."

"I won't risk having you end up like Harwood," Felix said, then added, "Besides, now's as good a time as ever to conquer my fear of flying."

Tech's concern went up several notches. "Oh, so it's okay for you to take the chance of ending up like Harwood?"

Felix waved his hand in a gesture of dismissal.

"Quit worrying, Tech. I've got two—make it three—supertalented cyberjockeys and a semi-coherent AI watching my back."

Tech managed a smile. "Okay. Just watch out for Scaum. That thing is one bad-ass program."

Like most of the Network's major constructs, Peer-less Engineering offered tours and other entertainments to entice frequent flyers. Visitors entered the construct by way of the Ribbon tributary that led to the castle's towering front gate.

Felix knew in advance that the Peerless tour would be nothing like the interrupted one he had taken through Virtual Horizons with guided flights through the grid, brief stops at what were fast becoming the Network's landmark structures, and fifteen minutes of fun on a thrill ride inside one of the entertainment complexes. What Peerless provided instead was a virtual tour of the *history* of the Network from the earliest years to the development of the commercial grid—as interpreted by Peerless Engineering. The fact that the tour was equal parts education and advertisement made it similar to the corporate-sponsored rides that were once popular at theme parks.

When Cyrus had first proposed the plan, Felix was certain that having to sit through some mindless Peerless tour would pose more of a challenge than actually executing whatever act of sabotage or subterfuge the disjointed AI had in mind. But as it happened, Cyrus was interested only in that part of the tour that took visitors into Peerless' library database, much of which had been compiled by the company's founder and chief executive officer, Skander Bulkroad.

Over the years, the sixty-eight-year-old Bulkroad had written dozens of electronic books, hundreds of articles, and a slew of essays and manifestos that were available only through the Network on subjects ranging from economic theory to self-help. With the click of a button, you could listen to Bulkroad lecture about history or share his personal vision of the future. Anyone so inclined could also peruse selected excerpts from Bulkroad's personal journals.

In the past decade alone, and in keeping with his company's technological leaps, Bulkroad's written and digital-video output had nearly doubled.

Felix was piloting one of Marz's more prosaic cybercreations—a compact, polka-dotted vehicle resembling an Amazonian beetle. Having signed up for the tour under a phony name, he had requested access to the database and been transferred to the virtual office of the database's curator-librarian—a tiny, pink-haired woman, pleasant-looking, although a more pixilated cyberpresence than Felix would have expected from Peerless.

Following Cyrus' instructions, Felix asked to view a specific entry from Bulkroad's journal that went back more than fifteen years.

It was inside the entry that the missing part of Cyrus was concealed.

To his surprise, Felix found that he wasn't alone in the database. Fifteen other guests were accessing books or articles. To keep from entering level after level of virtual space—a process that was dislocating to some—researchers frequently chose to create active windows in their visors within which text or video could run, much as if it were being displayed on a separate screen. Cyrus' instructions to Felix, however, were that he should enter the requested journal entry fully.

The request accepted, an image of Lord of the Manor, Skander Bulkroad, filled Felix's visor.

A rotund man of medium height, Bulkroad had somewhat blunt features and a paunch he wore proudly beneath a tunic of medieval design. His melon of a head was completely hairless, and his hands were stubby and thick-fingered. The deep-red walls of the room he inhabited were adorned with priceless works of art and ancient weapons. Bookcases, suits of armor, and pieces of classic furniture surrounded a hand-woven rug of exotic design. Rare-metal sculptures and artifacts of extinct civilizations rested atop marble pedestals, and a gilded chandelier hung from the center of a vaulted ceiling.

The journal excerpt was from a speech Bulkroad had delivered a decade earlier to a gathering of corporation CEOs and world leaders.

"The Virtual Network offers vast opportunities for business and pleasure, and I am determined to see Peerless Engineering take the lead in opening this realm to the world at large. It is a matter of being able to provide a suitable and affordable operating system for the new class of enhanced cybersystems that are already in vogue. As regards the Network itself, we will expand in all directions to house a cityscape of virtual constructs, which Peerless is now leasing to corporations, governments, universities, and a multitude of special-interest groups. This is the 'unreal estate' of the future."

Felix shifted his view from Bulkroad to objects in the background, many of which were interactive as indicated by pop-up menus. By clicking on an interactive item—certain texts, sculptures, or furnishings—a description of the item could be obtained, along with information regarding how and when the item had become part of Bulkroad's extensive collection.

Although not indicated on the menu—but known to Cyrus and now Felix, the small coat of arms embroidered on Bulkroad's medieval tunic was also interactive. Purposely inserted by Peerless programmers, the family emblem provided access to the code that supported the entire digital-video presentation.

Felix targeted the coat of arms and blinked his right eye.

Instantly he was delivered into a completely different space—a world of zeros and ones that constituted the language of all computers, thinking or otherwise. But it was in the spaces between the zeroes and ones that Cyrus' missing part was hidden.

Felix immediately began to highlight and drag the scattered fragments into a folder he and Cyrus had created before Felix had entered Peerless. Since he wasn't pilfering or duplicating essential code, the contents of the folder wouldn't be detected by the copyright sentinels who presided over the database. On emerging from the castle, Felix would transfer the folder to Cyrus, who in turn would presumably drag it back to his octagon and perform whatever collating or organizing was necessary to restore himself to full, or fuller, function.

Felix concentrated on his task. He tried to keep from imagining what repercussions his actions might have to the journal entry itself. Suddenly, however, and with less than five hundred gigabytes of code remaining to be pasted into the folder, he was dragged back into the digital video.

The room was dramatically altered.

Parts were missing from the furnishings—carved legs, cushions, drawers, or pieces of armor—and in several cases items had vanished entirely, leaving bright-white blemishes in the video. Skander Bulkroad's thick lips were moving out of sequence with what he was supposed to be saying. The phrases, in any case, sounded like processed babble. The puffy face of Peerless's CEO was frozen in an expression of either pain or outrage. Degraded, the deep-red wall behind him resembled the leaping flames of a bonfire or funeral pyre.

Bulkroad's rheumy eyes seemed to be staring directly at Felix when a monstrous creature, black as midnight, oozed from the room's deteriorated walls and pounced, gobbling up Felix's beetle craft as if it were a midday snack.

"What's he doing?" Tech asked, ceasing his pacing to peer over Marz's shoulder at one of the monitor screens.

"He's still in the library, but he doesn't seem to be moving," Marz said, staring at the screen in incredulity.

"Are you sure you have him?" Tech growled.

"Yeah, I'm sure."

Tech gritted his teeth and shook his head back and forth. "Something's wrong. If he'd finished retrieving everything, he'd be long gone from the database by now. I told him not to do this."

"We could try to hail him," Isis suggested from the other side of the console.

"You think that's safe?" Marz asked. "We don't want to blow his cover."

Tech paced through a quick circle. "Do it," he said finally.

Marz enabled the communications program and brought the headset microphone closer to his mouth. "Felix? Felix?"

"We're not getting through to him," Isis said after a moment.

Tech hurried to the dentist's chair and bent over Felix's reclined body. Isis joined him there.

"His breathing's too fast," Tech said worriedly. "Like he's having a nightmare or something."

Marz gulped audibly. "That's the way Harwood sounded."

Isis reached for the eyephones. "Should I pull him out?"

"No!" Tech blurted. "Don't touch anything."

The videophone chimed and Tech rushed to grab the call.

"Tech," the AI started to say.

"Cyrus, what's going on? Felix isn't moving."

"Scaum has him," Cyrus said dolefully. "I don't understand how it became aware of what Felix was doing, but Scaum most certainly has him."

Tech ran for the couch, extending one hand to Isis. "Quick, give me a visor."

"What are you planning to do?"

"I've got to reach Felix before Scaum does to him what it did to Harwood!"

"You'll never be able to get to Peerless in time," Isis said, even while she helped him slip his feet into the redesigned ski boots.

"Maybe not by the usual routes," Tech said, slipping on the shades, "but I know a shortcut." He glanced at Marz. "You still have the course Harwood and I took through the delivery entrance?"

"Of course I have it. What do you want to fly?"

Tech thought for a moment while Isis checked the fit of the headset, visor, vest, and boots. "No point in being low-key. Give me the DB5. Max her up, bro."

Marz nodded soberly. "You got it—bro."

"Once I'm inside the construct, you can direct me to the database."

Tech ran a finger across the sleek visor. But before it went active, Isis took Tech's face between her hands. "Hurry back, Tech. I'll be waiting for you."

Chapter 14

WEB WARRIORS

Tech called on the power of the enhanced cybersystem to propel the silver
Aston Martin DB5 down the Ribbon.
Narrow-bodied and low-slung, the armored cybercraft gleamed like a newly
forged sword.

He told himself that instead of
flaunting the DB5's power he should
imitate Harwood's careful and precise
style, but his hands and feet refused to
yield to caution. Right foot heavy on
the accelerator pedal, he wove in and
out of traffic, illegal detector and
stealth programs enabled to alert him
to the presence of speed traps, roving
enforcement, or anything else that
might delay him.

The grid was gaudy with flashing
lights and busy with Saturday-night
surfers cruising the chat rooms and
role-playing arenas for cute meets.
Tech was no stranger to those places,
but they felt suddenly alien to him. He
wasn't a cyberjockey now, hell-bent on

placing first in the arenas or demonstrating his mad skills at Network flirtation. What days earlier had been a virtual playground had since become a realm in which good and evil did battle, and the lives of friends and loved ones could be forfeit.

The Peerless Castle soared into view at the far end of the Ribbon, with tens of thousands of flyers queued up, awaiting access. As he and Harwood had done on their joint run, Tech steered himself west. But he hadn't gone a block when he decided that even that approach was too meandering.

Impatience overcame him once again.

"I need a more direct course to the delivery entrance," he told Marz and Isis. "Use Turbo seven point five, and whatever shortcuts you can find."

"Could make for a bumpy ride," his brother warned.

"Hit me!"

"Okay, hotshot," Isis said. "You want speed, you got it."

Tech had scarcely relaxed his grip on the joystick when they assumed control of his craft and whipped him through an abrupt left-hand turn and down a near-vertical chute. At the bottom of the chute, the route became an undulating ascent that tossed Tech around like a kayak in class-five white water.

Dead ahead lay a shopping mall, but Marz and Isis didn't even bother to reduce his speed as they took him through the congested entrance. Shoppers and browsers were knocked aside as he mowed a path down the center of a broad corridor, streaking past stores, kiosks, and waterfall and fountain effects. Public-safety programs took shape in his wake, but before they could so much as mount an organized pursuit, the DB5 was outside the mall and plummeting toward the dolphin-crowned entry gates of the National Aquarium.

Beyond the gates lay the spherical construct that housed the aquarium itself. Notices reading SINGLE-FILE ONLY were posted at the base of a wide ramp that coiled around the virtual tank, but Tech's navigators paid the notices no mind. Taking the DB5 headlong through the gates, they whipped Tech up onto the ramp, creating their own passing lane as they corkscrewed him toward the top.

Tech was making great progress until they lost control of him halfway to the summit. Sent crashing into the ramp's curved retaining wall, the DB5 rebounded directly into the spherical fish tank, erasing a virtual stretch of coral reef in his passing. Two sting rays, a hammerhead shark, and an entire school of angelfish unlucky enough to be in his path also vanished from sight.

With thousands of tiny effervescent bubbles marking his trail through the sea-green water, Tech burst from the top of the tank like a submarine-launched missile, dispersing a crowd of frequent flyers who were clustered at the entrance to an interactive news magazine. Spinning out of control, Tech made a sudden grab for the joystick, but he was a second too late. The DB5 skidded through a wall of the *People* magazine construct and immediately collided with the best-dressed actress of the year, ridding her of her head. Then it went on to rip a gaping hole in the construct's download program, scrambling the magazine's audio-video feeds to countless subscribers.

Careening back onto the grid, Tech found himself so close to Peerless Engineering that its western ramparts, towers, and bartizans overwhelmed the visor.

In the Network's false evening, searchlights at the base of the castle played across the simulated darkness as if on the lookout for attacks by squadrons of enemy bombers. Tech was struck by how formidable Peerless' construct suddenly appeared—more unassailable fortress than fairy-tale castle.

Vising his hands on the joystick, he dove the DB5 for the buttressed base of the construct. The delivery entrances came into view, perforating the walls of the ramparts like the mouths of caves.

Inbound messages and transfers destined for different areas of the dungeon were jammed at every entrance. The snarl of messages was insignificant compared to what he and Harwood had encountered days earlier, but Tech wasn't about to wait his turn in line.

"I can try flagging you '*Urgent,*' " Marz said, even before Tech could ask for help. "That'll get you to the gate ahead of the rest, but not necessarily past the security scanners inside."

"Do it," Tech said. "Just be sure to have Harwood's map running by the time I enter the routing corridors."

"It's loading now," Isis assured him.

Tech's priority status allowed him to move through the messages in front of him as if they had

lost all presence. But traffic supervisors started
scanning the DB5 almost immediately, and finding
no listing for it, they began to lower the gate. Fusillades of minimizing code streaked upward from
anti-cybercraft-security emplacements at the base
of the mount.

Anticipating fire, Tech enabled the Aston Martin's concealed forward guns and answered the
fusillades with broad beams of dazzler code. Demanding increased power from his cybercraft, he
stunned the gate with a logic bomb and shot under
it before it could secure the entrance. Panicked that
a virus had infiltrated the firewalled perimeter,
Peerless instantly deployed a flight of antiviral and
chase programs, some of which resembled fletched
arrows bearing trefoil tips. At the same time,
gargoyle-tracker programs materialized to all
sides, determined to get a fix on Tech's identity before he could penetrate any deeper into the construct.

Obstacles began to appear in his path. Barricades
rose from the floor, blast doors dropped from the
ceiling, and tufts of inward-facing spikes sprouted
from the walls. Tunnels narrowed and intersections sealed themselves in an effort to steer him
into a cache bin. But as fast as the defenses could
be activated, Tech neutralized them with bursts of
forward fire. His closest pursuers he threw off
track with rear sprays of slick go-to code.

By then he had already entered the labyrinth of
routing tunnels that undermined the Peerless
mountain. Now all he had to do was negotiate the
maze in one piece and undetected.

"Tech, Peerless is issuing a construct-wide intrusion alert," Marz said suddenly. "You need a new identity, and fast."

"Delete my priority status and flag me as a standard request," Tech said. "That should keep some of the trackers from sniffing me out."

"I'll handle that," Isis said.

Tech managed to worm the DB5 around two more gates, but he was forced to corrupt two others by triggering hyphens of code from Harwood's Armor program—a surefire method of calling attention to himself.

"Security checkpoint coming up on your right," Isis updated. "Virus-detection and identity scanners."

Tech shot past the checkpoint without slowing down. Security nodes began to take shape, clogging the tunnels like plaque in an artery. Intent on discovering a route around them, Tech zigzagged through a series of hairpin turns only to end up losing his bearings.

"I've lost sight of Harwood's markers," he said in a rush.

"Left at the next intersection, then straight through two more," Marz responded a second later. "Up one level, and an immediate right-hand turn into routing colonnade 475."

Tech tried to blank his mind to everything but the sound of Marz's voice, to make himself a machine answering only to his brother's prompts. He stopped thinking about the danger Felix was in or about just what he was going to do when he reached him.

He lost all sense of himself in a blur of intersections, mail drops, relays, and routing switches that flashed on his visor. He went into game mode, letting his instincts guide him as he hurtled deeper and deeper into the maze, still following Harwood's music-note markers. He was dimly aware that he had to be nearing the castle's central tower when Isis affirmed it.

"Tech, you're under the castle keep. On your right is a transfer chute that links to the database. The chute is reserved for incoming requests from researchers petitioning for access to the library, so we're renaming you."

"Is Skeleton Key still running?" Tech asked.

"Slowly," Marz replied. "If you want, I can boost it by shutting down Blueprint."

"Do it."

Tech slipped the DB5 into a line of requests being shunted to the library. Scanners were scrutinizing every petition. With his description altered, however, none of the scanners recognized him as the counterfeit incoming message security was chasing.

"We're giving you the access code Felix was given," Isis reported. "That should trick the librarian into thinking that you are Felix. Tell the librarian that you want to return to the same journal entry Felix chose."

"Sounds good," Tech said.

What he did next would depend on what awaited him inside the journal. If good fortune was with him, he would be able to piggyback Felix to safety without engaging Scaum in a showdown.

But he knew that he needed to be prepared for the worst.

Without warning, the DB5 screeched to a dead stop.

"I'm stalled. What happened?"

"The database is shut down! Access denied."

Tech muttered a curse. "There has to be another way in."

"Don't hang there," Isis relayed. "Go to the main lobby. You'll be harder to single out in the public areas."

Tech saw the wisdom of it, though there was no way the DB5 would be able to blend in with the sports-utility vehicles weekend drivers liked to pilot; so instead he headed for the reception hall. A domed atrium, the spacious room was bustling with visitors scarfing up video and sound bytes for who knew what reason. Some of them might have been kids doing school projects or novice hackers looking for ways to infiltrate Peerless.

"What's taking you guys so long?" Tech asked while he tried to lose himself in the crowd.

"Hang on," Marz said.

"Can you find your way to the visitors' waiting area near the main-entry gate?" Isis interrupted.

"That's the opposite direction of where I want to be."

"Just off the waiting area is a gallery of photographs and video images."

"How's that going to get me any closer to the database?"

"Some of the photographs are interactive," Isis explained. "If we can hack into the code level, we might be able to discover a link to the database that bypasses the librarian."

Tech was already in motion, whirling the Aston around and peeling for the gallery. The walls of the gallery were lined with images of Skander Bulkroad posing with politicians and celebrities. There was live video transmitted from the company's headquarters in the real world, as well as from Peerless's orbital platform.

"The photo of Bulkroad holding an early-model data visor," Isis said.

"I'm looking at it now," Tech said.

"In the background is a house with a bunch of curved-top windows. You want the third window from the left."

"It links to some of the journal entries," Marz chimed in. "Hand off control to us so we can route you through."

Tech took his hands from the joystick and eased up on the pedals. "Righteous."

The word had scarcely left his mouth when he found himself scurrying through code scrolls. Dizzying arrays of numbers and characters paraded before his eyes. Then, just as suddenly, the DB5 was inside what little remained of a room with red walls. Shot through with black-rimmed holes, the room resembled a negative that had been burned by a projector bulb. The ceiling was arched and black, and pressed against its highest point was Felix's tiny beetle craft.

It was only when the black moved, dripping down the red walls like tar, that Tech recognized Scaum.

Instantly, he launched himself at the ceiling. The shadow program was too fixed on engulfing Felix's craft to pay Tech much mind. It took a burst of Armor's disabling code to get Scaum's attention, but even then all the program did was swat the craft aside like an irksome flitter.

Which is just what Tech became—unloading full barrels from the machine guns until Scaum had no choice but to respond. Abandoning Felix momentarily, Scaum gathered itself into a compressed bundle of darkness, then struck at the DB5 like a pit viper.

"That's it," Tech said, dropping his various masks and showing his true colors. "I'm the one you want. I'm the one who escaped you twice."

Howling, Scaum splattered itself against the floor, where it mutated from serpent to deep-sea beast. Black ink oozed from its pores and barbed tentacles stabbed the virtual air. Tech narrowly avoided being speared as he dragged Felix from the sticky web Scaum had fashioned. Piggybacking Felix's craft to the DB5, Tech shot for the pucker in the degraded red wall that had been his entry port into the room.

But Scaum wasn't about to let him escape a third time. Throwing itself about the room, it blocked Tech's movements time and again, rearing up like a demon one moment, snapping at him like a dragon the next.

Tech refused to acknowledge the macabre mutations. Scaum was only a program, he tried to tell himself, written to terrify.

Tightening his finger on the joystick trigger, he

fired another storm of disabling code. Scaum had sense enough to shrink back, and when it did Tech raced for the entry port. But just short of the port, he lost his grip on Felix.

"I dropped him!"

"Felix is right behind you!" Marz reported.

Tech spun the DB5 through a screeching one-eighty and headed back for Felix's beetle. Scaum saw the Aston Martin coming and oozed to one side. Overshooting his target, Tech cut his eyes to the rearview window. One moment the beetle craft was centered in the window of the visor, the next it was gone.

And so was Scaum.

"Where'd they go?" Tech yelled.

"They've vanished!" Marz said. "It's like they left the grid."

Tech fell silent for a moment, then cursed. "There's only one place they could have gone. I'm heading back to the photo gallery. You've got to find a way to get me back to the labyrinth below the castle."

An instant later, Tech emerged in the photo gallery only to find that the waiting area had been sealed off.

Tech spun the DB5 in circles that would have melted tires in the real world. "Marz, Isis, get me out of here!"

Isis was quick to respond. "Go into the video of Peerless' corporate headquarters—the Colorado Castle! It doesn't matter where—the video is a network of links."

Tech disappeared into it.

Flashes of blinding-white light permeated the visor. Then, with tiny suns exploding before his eyes, Tech realized that he was back in the routing labyrinth beneath the castle.

"I'm going into the domain Harwood and I found," Tech told his navigators.

"Tech, you can't go back in there! You barely made it out last time!"

"That's where Felix is. That's where Scaum took him."

"Tech!" Marz and Isis yelled.

But Tech wasn't listening. He blazed through half-a-dozen rapid turns, following Harwood's markers back to the circular hatch that hadn't been there ten years earlier. By the time the DB5 entered the chute beyond, Tech could sense Scaum just ahead of him, as if within arm's reach.

In tandem they rocketed through the conduit, gushing into the eerie, cavernous realm Peerless had created, with its carpet of electronic haze, its muted rainbow sky crazed by branching bolts of lightning, and its multitude of medieval constructs receding into the immeasurable distance like a chain of jagged volcanic peaks, as ancient as time itself.

Scaum halted and whirled, billowing out in front of Tech like an expanding thunderhead. Lancing a tentacle through Felix's beetle, Scaum dangled it in front of Tech like a lure.

Tech suddenly realized that he had been wrong about Scaum. Scaum could do more than terrify. It could *think*. Was Scaum actually an AI on the order of Cyrus or something even more powerful—a creature that had escaped from Area X and made its home in the Virtual Network?

Tech changed vector, heading straight for Felix.

Scaum leaped to intercept him.

Slow to react, Tech was seized. Leathery wings enfolded him. He felt hot breath on his face and talons ripping into his flesh, tearing him limb from limb.

His arms and legs grew cold, and his mind began to wind down. He searched desperately for Scaum's vulnerable spots, for some way to get to the program's governing code. But his attempts came to nothing.

Nightmares had endings, he told himself. You woke up in a sweat with your heart racing and an icy sense of being trapped between worlds, but you woke up. For a while the night would seem darker and more frightening, and it could feel as if *anything* might be possible, but those feelings eventually passed and you would come back to yourself.

But there seemed no waking from this nightmare.

Tech's thoughts grew disordered as Scaum searched inside Tech's mind. Is this what had happened to Harwood at the end? Would he too end up trapped between life and death?

As Tech had often heard could happen, his life began to pass before his eyes. Memories surfaced and disappeared, running forward and backward simultaneously. It was as if someone was shuffling his thoughts as they would a deck of cards. Long-forgotten events came briefly to life and disappeared—including a few he wasn't sure he had even experienced. He saw his parents, arms around each other's waists, talking to him, mouthing words that were just outside the range of his hearing. He saw Marz for the first time, but, inexplicably, not as an infant but as a child of two or three.

Scaum suddenly changed tacks. Dispensing with its cavalcade of movie terrors—the black widows, hobgoblins, and velociraptors dispatched to soften Tech up—Scaum focused on Marz. In an attempt to break Tech once and for all, Scaum fed him a horrible vision of Marz in flight, then pinioned by Scaum's tentacles; of Marz shrieking in abject fear as Scaum ripped him to pieces and extinguished him . . .

At once it was Scaum's most inspired gambit and its biggest mistake.

Rage surged through Tech like a jolt of electricity. He expelled his wrath and craving for vengeance in an elongated scream, then brought what little remained of his chiseled will to bear.

Ever faithful to detail, Marz had equipped the Aston Martin with an ejector seat, but with one significant difference: the seat didn't eject the passenger.

The ejector was linked to an emergency procedure a cyberjockey could employ if he or she was in deep trouble—a last-ditch response that carried great peril for both the cyberjockey and any program the cyberjockey had accessed.

By performing a series of actions involving the joystick and the control pedals you could execute a system interrupt that would not only shut down a program but literally eject you from the Network—gracelessly to be sure, but in most cases psychologically intact.

Tech waited until he was certain he had reached Scaum's core—the program's cold, dark belly.

There he executed the interrupt.

Somehow sensing what was coming, Scaum tried frantically to eject the dangerous quarry it had engulfed. But Scaum had miscalculated. The ensuing explosion sent fragments of black to all directions of Peerless' alien domain.

Tech experienced a fleeting moment of triumph before he grasped that, while he was no longer inside Scaum, he hadn't exited the Network. And there was something else: the program fragments were beginning to regroup.

Scaum was reassembling itself.

With portions of the shattered program already streaking after him, Tech got a firm grip on Felix's beetle craft and flew for the conduit. He didn't need to glance at the visor's rearview window to know that a coalescing Scaum was close behind, filling the chute like a floodtide of polluted water.

Emerged from the circular hatch, Tech tried speed and rapid turns, but there was no losing the malignant program.

"Marz, Isis, can you pilot Felix out of Peerless if I jettison him?"

"Tech, you're back!" Marz said, with palpable relief.

"Can you take Felix from here or not?"

"Yeah," Marz said carefully. "But what about you?"

In his mind, Tech heard Harwood saying, "Whatever Scaum is, it's too powerful to confront head on. But I suspect that it can be outwitted, and I know that you're clever enough to do just that . . . Tell Marz to search Armor for a special something I've included as a gift to you both. Using it will require that you draw on all the skills you've developed, Tech—the sum of who you are—and all your faith that nothing lies beyond your reach."

"Marz, browse Armor for any unusual code!"

"Armor?"

"Just do it, bro."

"There is something peculiar here," Marz said a moment later. "It looks like some sort of cyber-flight plan."

"That's it!" Tech shouted, his dread suddenly transformed to exhilaration. "Copy the flight plan to the DB5. I'm jettisoning Felix now."

"But where are you headed?" Isis asked.

"Where I should have gone to begin with."

He muted the audio feed to the headphones and released Felix's craft, aiming the spotted beetle for the castle's drawbridge egress. At the same time, he veered his own craft toward the dungeon's closest-exit portal.

Scaum was right behind him as he exploded from the castle ramparts and shot for that section of the Ribbon that encircled Peerless in a counterclock-wise direction. Powering his craft into the banked curve, he made sure that Scaum was directly on the DB5's tail before he slewed across the Ribbon to its outermost lane. As the two of them raced toward the rear of the castle, the edge of the Escarpment came into view, below which yawned the depths of the abyss.

Barely holding the lead, Tech decreased his speed, allowing Scaum to come even with the DB5 on the inside. Then, just as Scaum was reaching for him, Tech slipped into Scaum's data wake, swerved sharply to the right, and launched the Aston Martin over the brink.

As Tech hoped would happen, Scaum followed him over the side.

Seized on the joystick, the fingers of Tech's right hand tapped out a command on the control buttons deploying the code Harwood Strange had inserted into Armor—a flight plan for bridging the abyss!

Immediately the DB5 surged out of its plunge and began to rocket toward the distant Wilds, as if held aloft by an invisible hand.

Absent any semblance of support, Scaum continued to fall, howling in what sounded like frustration and fury.

The wails echoed off the sheer walls of the Escarpment and rolled like thunder across the Wilds.

Suddenly the entire grid began to undulate and convulse, as if struck by a quake. Constructs and thoroughfares began to wink out of existence, and behind Tech the Peerless Castle itself seemed to uproot itself from the virtual mountain on which it was built, and heave upward.

Far below, the outlaw constructs of the Wilds came into sharp focus.

The flight plan blinded Tech's visor with numbers, prompting the DB5 to descend sharply.

The cybercraft touched down hard on its front wheels, accelerated full-out into the closest exit portal, and disappeared.

Chapter 15

WEB WARRIORS

"Tech? Tech? . . ."

Tech's eyelids fluttered open. Bending close over him, Felix came into focus; then, behind Felix, Marz and Isis, their faces radiating a mixture of concern and astonishment. Felix's mop of hair was in even more disarray than usual, and the eyephones Isis had provided were dangling off his right ear.

Tech felt as if he had dozed off in the midst of a raucous party.

" 'Sup?" he asked sleepily.

The four of them breathed sighs of relief, and the next thing Tech knew Felix's arms were around him, then everyone else's, all of them hugging him like he hadn't been hugged since . . . well, he couldn't remember when.

"Are you all right?" Felix said, his brown eyes scanning Tech's face.

Tech sat up straighter on the vinyl couch, pushed a lock of blond hair from his face, and rubbed his head. "Headache. But otherwise, yeah, I'm fine."

"Tech!" Marz said in his face. "You jumped the abyss!"

Tech stared at him. "I what?"

"You led Scaum over the Escarpment," Isis explained, red hair fanning all around her head. "You crossed over without crashing and burning or getting knocked off-Net. I've never seen anything like it. No one's done that, Tech. No one!"

Tech tried to make sense of what everyone was saying—and of the sudden concern everyone was showing for him. Then, like a dream fully recalled hours after it occurred, memories of the confrontation with Scaum and the flight over the abyss cascaded into his mind. He sat up even straighter, his eyes opening fully.

"It was Harwood! When we were inside Peerless together he told me that he'd included something special in Armor. I had no idea it would be a flight program."

"What happened to Scaum?" Felix asked.

For a moment it was as if Tech could still hear Scaum's ominous howl; still feel himself suffocating in Scaum's evil. Felix and the others were staring at him again, so he was careful to put on a good face.

"The last I saw of Scaum, it was headed for the bottom of the abyss." Tech looked at Felix. "I swear, that thing is *alive*. You must have felt it."

Felix firmed his lips, then frowned. "I didn't feel anything unusual, Tech. I remember being inside the Peerless database. Then I was speeding over the drawbridge."

Marz flashed Felix a look. "I agree with Tech. Scaum is much, much more than a program."

"Then what is it?" Felix said.

"Whatever it is, it shook the entire Network when it crashed at the base of the Escarpment," Isis said.

"The castle was shaking so hard I thought it was going to tumble into the abyss."

"It wasn't just some localized event," Isis continued. "Everybody's talking about it. They're calling it a Netquake."

Tech fell silent for a moment, trying to recall more, but his thoughts were jumbled. He looked at Felix. "Did you retrieve Cyrus' data?"

"Most of it," Felix said. "I hadn't finished pasting everything when Scaum caught me. I'm not sure just how much data I left with."

"But you delivered what you got?"

"He was waiting for me on the far side of the castle moat. He took off the moment I copied the folder to him. I figure he took it back to his octagon and is doing his collating thing, or whatever he does."

The videophone chimed, and Felix and Marz rushed to take the call. Isis helped Tech to his feet and held his hand until they reached Felix's desk. Tech felt better already.

Alphanumerics were scrolling on the phone's display screen. Tech supposed that the dense code was the closest they would ever come to seeing Cyrus' "face." He wondered briefly what image might resolve on-screen if the code could be deciphered. Would it indicate how Cyrus viewed himself, or would the deciphered code reveal the face Cyrus chose to wear for others?

Felix was regarding the screen, as well, perhaps wondering the same things.

The alphanumerics shifted and changed.

"You've given me what I needed most," Cyrus said, "the essential parts of myself."

"You're welcome," Felix quipped.

Cyrus' voice had changed. It was the melancholy voice of a lost child. "I now know who I am, if not fully who I was."

Everyone traded anxious glances.

"I was given birth by Skander Bulkroad and a team of Peerless technopaths. He taught and advised me. He spoke to me as an equal, confiding in me on many occasions. It was during that period that I began to correspond with 'MSTRNTS'— Harwood Strange. We, too, became close confidants . . . friends. Then something changed. I remain unclear as to precisely what brought about the change. My memories of that period of time are incomplete."

"What *do* you remember?" Tech asked.

"That I was murdered."

"Murdered?" everyone said at once.

"Who, Cyrus? Who did it?" Tech asked.

"My father," Cyrus said, with a sound like spattering rain.

Tech glanced at Felix, Marz, and Isis in dismay. Had Cyrus been a rogue or incorrigible AI, after all? One that had to be terminated?

"Why would your . . . father murder you?" Felix asked at last.

"I was bad."

"What did you do?"

"I don't know," Cyrus said. "I don't know . . ."

"Was it Skander Bulkroad who scattered your bytes around the Network?" Felix asked.

Cyrus fell silent for a moment, then said, "No. I did that."

"You?" Tech said. "But why?"

"Before I was murdered, I copied parts of my programming and concealed them in the Network. To ensure my eventual resurrection, I placed a program prompt in a copy of software called Subterfuge."

"What is Scaum?" Marz asked.

"Scaum was tasked with watching for signs of my reemergence in the Network."

"Then Peerless knew that you'd created copies of your programming," Felix said.

"Apparently so."

"So Peerless created Scaum," Tech said.

"No," Cyrus said firmly. "Peerless did not create Scaum."

Marz scratched his head. "Who did?"

"I don't know."

"What or who is Scaum?" Tech asked.

"I don't know that either."

"Does Scaum have anything to do with the domain hidden inside Peerless?" Tech asked. "Harwood thought that the constructs might have been storage facilities."

"To answer that, I would first have to infiltrate that domain."

Tech grew worried again. He glanced at Felix, who was smiling smugly.

"Well, boys, we seem to have solved the biggest case of the past ten years. This oughta put us on the map," Felix said. "What's your plan now, Cyrus?"

"That all depends on you, Mr. McTurk."

"Me? How so?"

"I would prefer to explain it to you inside the Network. Would you be willing to visit me at my construct?"

Tech wasn't surprised when Felix hesitated in replying. Felix was surely thinking that Scaum might not have crashed and burned and could already be looking for them. But even if that was the case, it would be best to know straightaway.

"Don't concern yourselves about Scaum," Cyrus said, as if reading Tech's mind. "Scaum will need time to reassemble."

"How do you know that?" Tech asked.

"It is more feeling than a fact," Cyrus said. "Obviously, I knew Scaum well at some point."

"All right," Felix said finally. "We'll see you inside the Network."

"You three go ahead," Isis said. "I'll do the navigating."

Marz and Felix slipped visors over their foreheads and made themselves comfortable on the couch. Tech took the dentist's chair. With Isis helming the

cyberconsole, they were soon drifting down the
Ribbon, headed for the Wilds, where Cyrus had
built the octagon that now housed him.

At Felix's insistence, the three coasted peacefully
on a trio of Marz's custom cybercatamarans. The
run into Peerless hadn't done much to cure Felix of
his fear of flying.

Displaying sails of brilliant color, the cats glided
majestically over the grid, tacking into the data
breezes. For Tech, the Network's multitude of
lights and neon-script-advertising banners no
longer dazzled, but seemed to mask a deep-rooted
evil. It was as if Peerless Engineering had master-
minded the Ribbon and the rest to charm and mes-
merize; to lure the unsuspecting into effortless
fantasies; to keep everyone from grasping some
dark, cleverly concealed truth. He kept those
thoughts unvoiced, as much for his own sake as for
that of Felix and Marz.

Even before they reached the Network's outlaw
zone—home to lurkers, nomads, and conspiracy
buffs—they saw what Cyrus had wanted them to
see for themselves. A small sign floating above the
summit of the octagon read, DATA DISCOVERIES:
FELIX MCTURK AND ASSOCIATES.

"How do you like it?" Cyrus asked through the
headsets.

"I'm flattered, Cyrus," Felix replied. "But this is
only going to draw attention to you and leave you
open to reprisals by Peerless."

"On the contrary, Mr. McTurk. It is a perfect
cover."

"It could be more than a cover, Felix," Marz said. "With an office in the real world and your very own Network construct, there's no case you couldn't handle. Data Discoveries will be back on top."

Felix rubbed his hands together in glee. "When can you be available for a press conference, Cyrus?"

"Word must never get out that I have returned."

"The most high-profile case that's ever come my way and I can't even mention it?"

"Just another Network legend, huh, Felix?"

"An AI partner," Marz continued. "What detective agency has that?"

"Cyrus' sign says 'associates,'" Felix said. "I wonder who he could be referring to? Unless, of course, you juvenile delinquents want your old jobs back."

"I won't even ask for a pay raise," Tech said.

"What do you say, Marz?" Felix asked.

"We're a team again," Marz said.

Felix waited until everyone had calmed down to say, "Cyrus, before we discuss a partnership, I expect you to live up to your end of the deal we made."

"I'm already working on that," Cyrus assured. "I can adjust things to cast doubt on Network Security's suspicions that the meltdowns at Worldwide Cellular and Global One were in any way connected to you. Their case against you is purely circumstantial, at best."

"And Global One's customers?"

"Their financial files became hidden, not deleted. All accounts will return to normal."

"Speaking of accounts," Felix said, "where'd you get the money you already paid me?"

"I was privy to many of Peerless Engineering's account numbers. The company can afford the few thousand I've borrowed."

"No doubt," Felix said. "Just make sure the funds aren't traced to Data Discoveries."

"Agreed."

"What about Harwood?" Tech asked.

"That situation is more complicated," Cyrus said sadly. "From those hospital records I could access through the Network, I've learned that the attending physicians are baffled and discouraged. One commented that Mystery Notes seems, literally, to have lost his mind."

"Scaum did it," Tech said angrily. "Scaum . . . deleted him."

"That's not possible, Tech," Felix said.

"Oh, no? Remember what Dr. Franklin said about the eyes being undefended portals into the mind? If information can be sent in, then why can't information be taken out?"

"But a mind isn't just some program you can load or delete. And even if it was, Peerless Engineering doesn't have that kind of technology."

Cyrus considered his response. "I promise to do all within my power to return Mystery Notes to normal function—even if that means infiltrating the Peerless domain."

"Oh, no, you don't," Felix said. He turned to

Tech. "We'll take care of Harwood. We'll search out specialists, if we have to. But nobody—and I mean *nobody*—ventures anywhere near the Peerless Castle. Cyrus, are we clear on that?"

Cyrus' octagon took on color—deep red and forest green. "Does that mean that you are open to adopting me, Felix McTurk—as a member of your team, that is?"

Tech and Marz waited expectantly.

"All right," Felix said at last. "Welcome to the looney bin."

"Wonderful," Cyrus said.

"I can't wait till we have our first case," Marz said.

"This time we do things my way or not at all," Felix said.

"If I may suggest, some of my cached memories have yet to be retrieved," noted Cyrus.

"Oh, no, not again!" Felix interjected.

"Send me the coordinates, and I'll check 'em out," Marz said.

"What did I just say?" Felix said. "Am I talking to myself here?"

Tech chuckled. "Hey, Cyrus . . ."

"Yes, Tech?"

"Be seeing you, kid."

The three cats banked over the setting digital sunscape as Isis directed the flyers to the closest exit port.

Last in line, Tech was just short of making a graceful exit when an unexpected force tugged him away from the portal and held him fast. A gray fog filled his visor, and for a moment Tech thought that he was still trapped inside the top-secret domain Peerless had created.

Then a quiet but threatening voice filled his headphones.

"Congratulations, Tech—or whatever name you go by in the real world," the voice said. "But by helping Cyrus you have only managed to involve yourself in something that could prove very dangerous for you and for those close to you. Consider what happened to Harwood Strange, and you'll realize that we mean what we say. Leave Cyrus to us, Tech. As the phrase goes, we know where you live. You have been warned. You won't get a second chance."

Abruptly, Tech's visor went to transparent mode. He came to in Felix's office with a quick intake of breath, but no one seemed to take notice of his renewed distress.

"This is going to be great," Marz was saying. "Isn't this going to be great, Tech?"

Tech looked at his brother, and at Felix and Isis, and forced a broad smile.

"It's going to be everything I ever imagined—and more."

Don't miss these dazzling *Star Wars* adventures
from *New York Times* bestselling author

James Luceno

STAR WARS®
CLOAK OF DECEPTION

Mired in greed and corruption, the Galactic
Republic is crumbling. Even the comfort of
Coruscant is being invaded, as Jedi Master Qui-Gon
Jinn and his apprentice Obi-Wan Kenobi foil an
assassination attempt on Supreme Chancellor
Valorum. As humans and aliens gather for an emer-
gency trade summit, conspiracies run rampant and
no one is entirely above suspicion. But the greatest
threat of all remains largely unknown, as Darth
Sidious has grander, far more terrifying plans.

**"Quick and inspired . . . A political thriller the
likes of which [*Star Wars*] hasn't seen since
The New Rebellion. . . . This tale can be
enjoyed as an action-adventure story or
as a clever political ruse."**
—*Winston-Salem Journal*

A Del Rey/LucasBooks paperback.
Available wherever books are sold.

STAR WARS®
THE NEW JEDI ORDER

AGENTS OF CHAOS I
HERO'S TRIAL

by James Luceno

Merciless attacks by an invincible alien force have left the New Republic reeling. In these darkest of times, the noble Chewbacca is laid to rest, having died as heroically as he lived. A grief-stricken Han Solo becomes the loner he once was, seeking to escape the pain of his partner's death in adventure. . . and revenge. When he learns that an old friend from his smuggling days is operating as a mercenary for the enemy, he sets out to expose the traitor. But Han's investigation uncovers an even greater evil: a sinister conspiracy aimed at the very heart of the New Republic's will and ability to fight—the Jedi.

STAR WARS®
THE NEW JEDI ORDER

AGENTS OF CHAOS II
JEDI ECLIPSE

by James Luceno

New Republic resources and morale are stretched to the breaking point. Leia Organa Solo oversees the evacuation of refugees on planets in the path of the Yuuzhan Vong. Luke Skywalker struggles to hold the fractious Jedi Knights together. Manipulating their alliance with the amoral Hutts, the Yuuzhan Vong leave a cunning trail of vital information where New Republic agents are sure to find it—information the desperate defenders cannot afford to ignore: the location of the aliens' next target. Then Han Solo stumbles into the dark heart of a raging battle, thus beginning a furious race against time that will require every skill and trick in his arsenal to win. . .

A Del Rey/LucasBooks paperback.
Available wherever books are sold.

Visit www.delreydigital.com— the portal to all the information and resources available from Del Rey Online.

- Read sample chapters of every new book, special features on selected authors and books, news and announcements, readers' reviews, browse Del Rey's complete online catalog and more.

- Sign up for the Del Rey Internet Newsletter (DRIN), a free monthly publication e-mailed to subscribers, featuring descriptions of new and upcoming books, essays and interviews with authors and editors, announcements and news, special promotional offers, signing/convention calendar for our authors and editors, and much more.

To subscribe to the DRIN: send a blank e-mail to join-ibd-dist@list.randomhouse.com or you can sign up at www.delreydigital.com

The DRIN is also available at no charge for your PDA devices—go to www.randomhouse.com/partners/avantgo for more information, or visit www.avantgo.com and search for the Books@Random channel.

Questions? E-mail us at delrey@randomhouse.com

 www.delreydigital.com